MARS
VERSUS
MAPLE SCHOOL

by
Nick DiMartino

University Book Store Press
Seattle, Washington

MARS VERSUS MAPLE SCHOOL
Copyright © 2012 by Nick DiMartino

Anna Micklin, publishing coordinator
Jake Monderen, cover design
Brad Herst, technical consultant

UNIVERSITY BOOK STORE PRESS
Espresso Book Machine
First Printing: June 2012

All rights reserved.

ISBN: 978-1-937358-14-3

UNIVERSITY BOOK STORE
4326 University Way NE
Seattle, Washington 98105
www.ubookstore.com
206-634-3400

For autographed copies, with free shipping, call:
206-543-5896

"Let the biographer print fully, completely, accurately, the known facts without comment; then let him write the life as fiction."
--Virginia Woolf

"Come out naked and God will dress you."

-- Algerian proverb

for
my father
ERNESTO DIMARTINO

PART ONE

Chapter 1
Fifty Years Later

Not a trace of it remains.

I didn't realize that last Sunday, as we were driving home from a family brunch at my brother's golf and country club. On impulse I begged my nephew to take the old exit off the freeway into south Seattle.

"Do you mind? Do you have a lot of homework? Just for a second." We got off at Columbian Way and followed it until it turned into 15th and then all the way down to the familiar turn-off at Pearl Street, and up the hill.

"That's where we used to live," I said as we came down the other side, pointing at a rambler of dusty faded brick on the corner. "Your father and I, when we were kids. Can we stop for a second? You can park over there."

My nephew pulled up on the side of the hill by the mailbox. I tried not to peer too obviously through the windows to see who was living there now. It used to seem so much bigger when we lived in it. Nothing alive was moving inside, as far as I could see. The shrubbery was sadly overgrown, the lawn infested with dandelions and no longer neatly edged, the flower beds surrounding the house bare and twiggy and strangled in weeds.

"They've really let it go," I said. "It would break Dad's heart to see this." My father used to keep his gardens gorgeous and immaculate. Every year when his rhododendrons were in bloom the neighbors would slow down as they drove past our corner.

But it wasn't our old house I had come here to see. That wasn't the point of this little detour into the past.

"I'll wait for you here," said my nephew, turning up the volume of the car radio and unfastening his seat belt to make himself more comfortable.

"I'll be right back."

I closed the car door and started walking down the familiar stretch of sidewalk, past houses once so alive with delights and terrors, now shrunken and old and almost comic in their harmlessness. Where the Johnsons had lived, and the Hiraharas, and the Withrows. Past the Bergamini house on the corner where Sandra had lived, the prettiest girl at our school

– Sandra, who had once been my friend. Past steep, sinister Dawson Hill, which we had been so strictly forbidden to ride down on our bikes, now looking not nearly so dangerous. And I continued walking one more block past Dawson, already aware that something was disconcertingly wrong, doubting my memories, my steps faltering until they came to a dead stop where the cyclone fence should have surrounded and protected the upper playfield.

There was no fence. There was no playfield.

The neighborhood street simply continued on with houses and yards I didn't remember, as though there had never been basketball hoops and baseball diamonds, as though I had just imagined a pale yellow brick-and-wooden two-storey schoolhouse with a row of five portable classrooms along the eastern border of the lower playfield. Nothing remained to even hint that such a thing could ever have been true, that Maple Elementary School ever existed, as though it had been snatched up in a cosmic bubble and whisked away into outer space, out of people's minds and memories.

But it was here once, all right. When we moved into our new house, Maple School was very real and became our new school and the beginning of our new life. It swallowed me and changed me and left its mark on me, particularly during my fifth grade year when I was eleven years old. When you're born on the eleventh day of the eleventh month, the year you turn eleven is a special one, and mine was destined to be one of enormous discoveries…

"Everything okay, Unc?"

I realized I was still standing on the corner, staring at a house where the schoolyard should have been, driving a little spaniel wild inside the front window, who was barking hysterically at the ominous stranger.

"Oh, right. Sure, everything's fine."

I became aware of my nephew's hand on my shoulder, trying to bring me back to my senses. He had walked down the two blocks to where I was standing stranded on the corner like a man who has lost his contact lens, blinking and stupefied, trying to see something that's no longer there.

"Not the way you remember it?"

"No," I had to admit. "No, it's not. Not at all."

He waited for me to go on, and when I didn't, said, "Come on, Unc. Before you get too wet."

Not until then did I realize raindrops were sliding down my forehead and cheeks. I was completely unaware that it was raining. We walked back to his car before it started coming down hard.

Staring into the windshield wipers on the long drive home, I fell into a tired trance and found myself remembering.

Something happened to me in 1957 when I was in the fifth grade at Maple School, something that changed my life. Or maybe it was many little things all happening at once, having a cumulative effect. Ever since the day I discovered Maple School was gone I've been clutching at all the little details that I can drag back from the flabby, worn-out folds of my memory. It all happened over fifty years ago – how foggy and fragmentary those memories seem today! – and to make matters worse my perceptions are filtered through the limited understanding of an eleven-year-old boy who was trying very hard to believe that the world made sense and was a good place, half the time not paying attention, half the time misunderstanding.

This would be the year I woke up, the year I began discovering that I was not the good boy I always thought I was, that some of my feelings upset people, that some very real parts of me were unacceptable and best kept to myself, especially to be guarded from my parents but really, I could trust no one. I started keeping secrets. An unpredictable, frightening new me was awakening along with the new hair disconcertingly appearing on my body.

By the time I was eleven I knew that what normal boys experienced with girls and sports and cars I could only desperately imitate, hoping I could catch on or bluff my way through without anyone realizing I was faking it.

That was the year where I failed at faking it. That was the year I started to become real, whether I wanted to or not. That was the year I became a writer.

Chapter 2
The Call of the High Wires

When I was ten years old my parents bravely invested all of their savings into building a modest little dream-house in South Seattle. It meant moving away from the place I had always known as home, our Beacon Hill apartment with its backyard and swing-set just on the other side of the hedge from the brick home of Nana, my father's mother.

My grandmother was an old-fashioned woman who, when she wasn't cooking or cleaning or crocheting by her stove, spent most of her time outdoors, with flower gardens all around her house and a huge vegetable garden behind it. There her grandsons could wander down orderly rows of tomatoes and beans, leafy green aisles of romaine and spinach, bounded by briars of raspberries and boysenberries, a kingdom ruled by its own laws and customs, where Nana reigned in kerchief and rubber boots. One of six brothers and sisters, my grandmother grew much of the food that ended up on the dinner table. She frequently hosted huge family gatherings for our uncles and aunts and cousins over the holidays.

I adored Nana. I basked in her attention. She blatantly favored me of her two grandsons, to my brother's frequent annoyance. Named after her adored husband, who had tragically died at the age of forty-one, her grandson could do no wrong. My namesake had been the single great love of her life, and now her eldest son had restored him to her in a boy with the same name, magically brought back to life in a new incarnation.

Losing the closeness of Nana was one of life's first blows to my self-confidence. That last day living on Beacon Hill I hugged her on the sidewalk in front of her home, crying and terrified as my child's mind grappled with the scary notion of what moving away might mean. From seeing her every day after school and helping her work in her gardens, from Saturday morning breakfasts, weekend matinees, and "parents' night out" sleepovers, from spending as much time at her house as at mine, I would be seeing her only once a week, on Sunday afternoon, the day set aside for Nana to join us for supper, where I would share her with the whole family until my father drove her home in the evening. We would never be alone together again.

Our new home on Pearl Street left me stranded, in a big new house with nowhere to go, separated from Nana, snatched away from the drug store on the corner and the little grocery store across the street, away from the Fonseca boys and the Belottis and all our other neighbors and the people we saw every Sunday at St Peter's Church, away from everything and everyone we knew.

I was nervous but mostly excited. I hadn't fallen in love with anyone yet, so friends seemed casual and plentiful and replaceable. But suddenly I was without anyone to play with.

Summer afternoons stretched out long and lonely. When my brother and I had exhausted each other's company, we would walk down to the school playground. He would always end up playing on someone's team.

I would watch. I didn't play physical games very well. I was clumsy, and lacked sufficient determination to beat anyone. I always preferred watching.

On several afternoons I noticed another boy who wasn't running about shouting with the others. He was sitting at the end of the bleachers, and to my delight he was usually concentrating on an open paperback. Finally it was that book in his hands that drove me to go up to him and ask what he was reading. He looked up, squinting into the sun, and showed me the cover.

"Ever read anything by Isaac Asimov?"

"No."

"It's one of his robot novels."

I sat down beside him, and with only a question or two of prompting he began explaining to me at length the laws of the robots.

His name was David Starr, and he was proud to have the same name as the brave young space ranger hero of Asimov's popular science fiction series. When I asked where he lived, he pointed. It was just across the street from the elementary school. We were practically neighbors, and the same age. We would both be in fourth grade next year.

He had red hair, a round face, and a hearty splash of freckles across his nose and cheeks. He didn't have a lot of personal things to say, but there was one thing he could do better than anyone. He loved to tell you the plots of science fiction stories. He knew dozens of them, and remembered all the complicated twists and turns, plot-point by plot-point. I had never read science fiction before. I didn't know who Isaac Asimov was, or Robert Heinlein, or Arthur C. Clarke.

David promptly introduced me to all his favorite authors, turning my reading life upside down. Suddenly I was reading paperbacks with thrilling covers written for adults.

I read Philip K. Dick. I read Clifford D. Simak and Alfred Bester and Edmond Hamilton. I couldn't get enough. As that summer slowly came to an end, to my parents' horror and strictly financed by my own hoarded allowance money, I joined the Science Fiction Book Club. I received my monthly book in the mail. I gobbled them all up, from moon colonies to time-travel to alternate universes.

But more than any other of the numerous science fiction subgenres, the one that seized hold of my imagination most was the whole concept of an alien intelligence. I'd never really considered what that might be like. Life forms completely different from us! A whole other way of thinking and perceiving... An entirely alternate value system... My poor human mind had to stretch to the breaking point to accommodate such outrageous thoughts.

This had one strange, oddly disturbing result.

Our new home was half a mile away from a snug little enclave of relatives all living on the same street, their gardens back to back – Auntie Jo, Auntie Carmie, and Auntie Rita. To get to their homes, you could walk from our house down to the main street, take a hike up 15th Avenue, and then trek back up to their houses – or, if you were a local and knew better, you could accomplish the same journey in half the time by taking a shortcut there in a direct line through neighborhood backyards.

The shortcut involved slipping between a couple of houses, dashing across a couple of patios, and then crossing an undeveloped field of tall wild grass. This field was the stumbling-block. When it got dark, it was scary. Power lines stretched overhead, supported across the field by three titanic pylons. A lumpy, crooked path of beaten earth crossed the wide, neglected property, winding through a pothole-infested terrain of stickers and vines. You entered it from the backyard of a house on one street and escaped from it through the backyard of a house two blocks down.

For the nimble of foot and sharp of eye, it was quick and easy.

On that particular day, after spending the afternoon with David Starr, up in his tight, cosy loft of a bedroom reading science fiction comics and the first three chapters of a terrifying little paperback called *The Invasion of the Body Snatchers*, I had come home at dinnertime, the borrowed paperback tucked under my arm, to find the house silent, the kitchen light on but no one there, and no sign of dinner. Propped up on the kitchen table was a note from my mother telling me to join her and my brother at Aunt Carmie's, where the aunties and a couple of their daughters had gathered that afternoon to play their favorite card game, *canasta*.

It was an easy walk, but which route would I take? Soon it would be dark, and after dark we never went through the empty lot. But it was just twilight, and though the path through that property was uneven and treacherous, I could still make my way with reasonable certainty, if I left right away. And it was so much shorter!

Leaving *The Body Snatchers* by my bedside to scare myself silly when I got home, I slipped on a light windbreaker, locked the back door, and set off up the street. Crossing through yards, creeping quietly between neighborhood houses, I could see families inside through lighted windows having dinner, and I realized I was hungry. By the time I got to the field, it was a little darker than I'd anticipated, and my pace picked up as I set off across it.

The evening was hushed and hot, the air crackling with tension, and every step through the grass caused a loud rustling in the stillness. I began to have the creepy feeling that I wasn't alone. If something bad happened and you screamed out there, would anybody hear you? Now I was practically running, while trying not to make a sound. I was so focused on listening to see if I could hear anyone following me, hurrying faster and faster through the thickets and weeds, that I missed a shift in the landscape, caught my foot on a half-underground root and fell headlong with a body-wrenching slam.

What I remember is the sudden stillness.

And then a soft hum. I didn't know where it came from. Those tall, alien-looking pylons seemed to guard the field, monoliths fifteen-stories high with wires that I could barely see. The hum was getting louder. It seemed to come from the wires.

I became irrationally terrified. Suddenly I had the gut-wrenching suspicion that I knew why I always felt so separate from everyone else. Why I was afraid to let anyone know what I was really thinking. I wasn't human. It was the obvious explanation. Suddenly all the pieces fit. The reason I felt so different from my parents and brother and other kids was because I *was* different, very different – an alien, planted here in a normal family so that I could pass as normal, pretending to be one of them. I was some kind of mimic from outer space. I was a pod person pretending to be human.

It all made sense. And now my time on earth had come to an end. That humming in the field was the voice of my people from across the universe. They were calling me back to the stars.

I ran all the way to Auntie Jo's.

I arrived sweaty and dirty and wide-eyed with terror. My hands were scratched and bleeding from my fall, and the knee of my pants was torn. I could just barely hold back the tears. With her happy little dogs yapping about her ankles, Auntie Jo took me into her spotless kitchen, where a heap of bowls and pans were dripping clean in the rack, and gave me a piece of her pizza straight out of the oven – Auntie Jo's pizza was the best, no other auntie's could compare with her thin crust baked in a rectangular tray with dark, rich sauce and cut into little squares with a single pepperoni slice in the middle of each piece. She laid a hot square in the palm of my hand.

One bite made me human again.

From then on, whenever I was alone, I walked the long way to my aunties' houses, down well-lighted 15th Avenue, never crossing through that field alone again, never daring to confirm the aching suspicion that my survival depended on remaining hidden, that I was a stranger to this planet, and that I was stranded here, alone.

I was determined to continue pretending to be human as long as I could.

Chapter 3
The Boy in the Mirror

Just who is this little alien boy who fears he isn't human? Let's take a look at my overweight young self still dripping from my shower as I stand in front of the big bathroom mirror, the glass damp and slightly fogged, staring at the bare softness of my insecure body beneath the bright overhead light, with a critical frown.

I'm just about to pull on my undershorts but pausing for this quick, bitter assessment. I never look in a mirror without cringing, but I always hope that maybe this time what I see won't be quite so disappointing. I never shower without afterward spending at least one dreadful moment locked in the small, steamy room examining my naked reflection. To my great anguish, I don't look the way a classic American boy is supposed to look. I consider this shortcoming my personal failing.

One glance at my naked ten-year-old reflection, and I groan miserably. It's everything I dislike in naked bodies. I have a shapeless belly without any definition and without any hint of a waist, framed by love handles. The dreaded Dr Rutherford has already let me know that I need to lose ten pounds. Ten pounds! I'm only ten years old and already worrying about my weight. I'm pudgy and unappealing, and now, to make matters worse, I'm starting to turn hairy. Why is this hair starting to grow on me? How can I stop it?

I'm staring with a grimace into the glass at the boy I see reflected there. He doesn't have much forehead, his eyelashes are too long, and his lips don't seem to go with his face. Not only that, but he's short and squat, like a little barrel with arms and legs. My mother tells me that I get my build from her, that she's short-waisted and that's why I'm short-waisted.

This gives me no comfort at all.

I used to be cute when I was little. I've seen photos. I was a child ring-bearer once in a wedding, a perfect little Italian boy in an immaculate white suit. I was a doll. Then my adorable brother was born. Suddenly all the little black-and-white snapshots show that I'm ten pounds heavier and wearing glasses that are always sliding down my nose, looking completely uncomfortable with myself, like I've been stuffed into a body that doesn't fit. Overnight, in an instant, I'm rendered homely and awkward, folding my arms across my chest to hide my gut, sucking in my stomach to make it go away, wearing my pants up too high in a desperate attempt to hide my tummy.

Buying new pants has become a nightmare. How I dread being dragged from one department store to another by my mother, trying on different brands, consulting an army of salespeople, searching for pants to accommodate my unusual frame. More than once I simply break down sobbing in the men's dressing room, surrounded by pants that won't fit.

"What's taking you so long?" calls my mother, on the other side of the door. "Have you tried them on yet? Come out, let's see how they look."

"I can't button them," I manage to say without choking.

"Suck in."

"I *am* sucking in."

"Well, you're the one who always wants that second piece of pie," she reminds me pitilessly. The solution is always the same. "Now, stop feeling sorry for yourself. We've got to find you a good pair of pants for school. Here, try on these." Another pair of pants is lowered down on top of me, over the dressing-room door. "Come on, put them on and let's see how they fit." Try on another pair, and then another, and then another, all too tight around the waist or too baggy around the legs or dragging on the ground. No longer wearing boys' sizes, which simply won't button shut. Now I've advanced into the sizes of a new category discreetly marketed as Husky. That's the commercial euphemism. It's the non-judgmental way of saying fat.

I quickly get on the scale and then jump off again, horrified. That merciless scale never lets me get away with anything! It's not fair, the way the numbers keep climbing up. I'm scarcely ten years old and I've become the ugly one, while my little brother two years younger is naturally trim and fit without even trying, looking exactly the way a young boy is supposed to look, athletic and confident and pleasingly proportional. Kids at school give me a knowing smile and tell me my little brother is so cute. This does not make me happy.

So begins my obsession with The Other who is all the things I'm not, naturally confident and slim and attractive. He first comes to life for me in a magazine photo. Once I've spotted him, I can't stop admiring him, a young man wearing only a posing brief, little more than a cup with strings, whose artfully posed body amid several broken Greek columns has been greased in a classic muscle pose.

That first photo is one of my life's greatest unsolved mysteries.

I don't remember why I was snooping through the drawers of Nana's bureau in her bedroom. For that matter, I can't remember why I was alone at Nana's house. I wasn't a snoop, and I was seldom left alone there. The situation is odd, to begin with. Prying wasn't my usual behavior. I may have been searching for the nightgown she once told me about, the kind designed in a more inhibited era to remain on the woman during intercourse, with a strategically placed hole for the only place of actual contact.

Instead of a funny nightgown, in the bottom drawer of my grandmother's bedroom bureau, under a pile of folders and papers and several framed photos, I discovered a magazine called *Male Physique* dated May 1943.

I'm still confounded remembering it. What was it doing there? I broke into a sweat looking through it. It couldn't possibly have belonged to my grandmother, but then who did it belong to? Slowly I turned the pages, staring in disbelief. Once I had seen it, I knew I had to have it. I slid it under my shirt to get it out of my grandmother's bedroom, and somehow got it out of the house.

If Nana noticed it was gone, she never admitted it. It was almost as though she were actually unaware of its existence as well as its disappearance. But then why would it have been there? In a family with two very heterosexual sons and a very heterosexual husband, who would have bought that magazine?

The answer to that question will never be known.

In that magazine, next to the photo which became my very first piece of pornography, was a far-fetched article about a Civil War miracle, a Confederate soldier who had been shot through the groin by a bullet which then impregnated a Union nurse. How often did I read that story while daydreaming over the treasured, stolen photo of the perfect young man.

Chapter 4
In Suits, at the End

My father worked in produce. That meant that he got up at four in the morning six days a week to drive down to Western Avenue where he was the manager of an assembly line of European immigrants in rubber aprons and rubber gloves washing and packaging vegetables for ten to twelve hours a day. If anyone was sick, he took their place. After long stretches of backbreaking labor, crating and storing and trucking, he often didn't get home till seven at night. Nevertheless, in spite of all his hard work, living frugally, cutting every corner, the cost of sending his sons to Catholic school was simply out of his reach.

So although as a family we now attended St. George's Church for Mass every Sunday, my brother and I did not attend St. George's School. Instead we went to the free, public and far more convenient Maple Elementary, just two blocks down the street from our home. As a consequence, so that the church could supplement our public school education with the religious doctrine we would be missing, my brother and I were expected to go to St. George's School every Saturday morning to attend special religion classes for public school kids. That way we would be able to receive the sacrament of Confirmation along with the kids attending St George's.

Receiving Confirmation was a mandatory sacrament for Catholics. You were being sworn in as a soldier of Christ. These inescapable preparatory sessions were called CCD classes. The initials stood for Confraternity of Christian Doctrine, whatever that meant, and they were taught on Saturday mornings, some classes by nuns, some classes by lay people, a blemish on the entire weekend.

Our class of fifteen fourth grade boys was taught by Mr Norwood, a fiftyish man with a military crewcut gone gray, long electric eyebrows he never trimmed, and icy blue eyes like steel cutters. He was tall, and walked rigidly erect, as though he had a broom handle for a spine. Most of the time, rather than sit at the chair behind his desk, he would come around and lean back against the desk behind him, inserting himself into the midst of us. He seemed to like this closeness, and talked to us in a soft, conversational style, as though we were his friends. Mr Norwood prided himself on understanding boys, and always addressed us with a smug confidence, as though he could see into our minds and knew our deepest secrets.

I remember one morning in particular, when we were a little rowdier than usual, well-rested and squirmy, full of ourselves and brimming with the unchanneled energy of youth, wanting to get CCD over with so that the weekend could officially get underway. Mr Norwood had to ask us several times to take our seats, and finally said to the few boys who were being most vocal, "Gentlemen, would you mind lowering your voices, please, and showing a little courtesy to the rest of us by taking your seats?"

With shuffling and snorting and a little smothered laughter, we assumed some semblance of order.

"Today, gentlemen, we're going to talk about the sin you commit when you're all alone and thinking about girls," he said. "You all know what I mean. Anybody want to tell me what that particular sin is called?"

We all froze in dread. It was far too early to say that word out loud and risk getting it wrong.

"Now, don't be shy. You all know the answer to that one. It's called many dirty things, but the real word for it is masturbation. You all knew that, didn't you? Everyone say the word with me. All together now: masturbation."

We all dutifully said the word.

"I've never known a boy who didn't know all about masturbation. So don't even pretend to me that you don't know *exactly* what I'm talking about."

I didn't know what he was talking about. I didn't masturbate. I hadn't figured out how to do it yet, but I wasn't going to admit that in a room full of boys my own age. He looked slowly around the room, directly into the guilty eyes of each and every one of us.

"I know what's on your mind. You've all got girls on the brain, just tell me you don't. How about you, Tucker?"

Tucker giggled.

"You don't say. And how about you, McGregor?"

"You know it, sir."

Embarrassed laughter from the rest of us.

"I know what happens to your body when you start thinking like that," persisted Mr Norwood. "And I know what your hand does when no one is looking – that naughty hand of yours. Ever have trouble with that hand, Johnson?"

"No, sir." Johnson blushed. "I mean, yes, sir."

"No use pretending, Johnson. And that's a sin, gentlemen. Abusing your God-given body for idle pleasure is a sin punishable in hell."

Though technically I hadn't figured out the actual physical maneuvers of masturbation, I did know how to stimulate myself, and a number of subtle ways to achieve that. When I was looking in my magazine, I knew that the flush of heat and the change in my genitals and the thoughts rushing through my head were what Mr Norwood would qualify as punishable.

"God sees you, gentlemen, even if nobody else does, and He is going to remind you in Heaven of every single time you do it."

I tried to swallow, without success. The very thought of a celestial tallying of my nighttime liberties was appalling. "Every time?" The words slipped out before I realized I'd said them out loud.

That was all Mr Norwood was waiting for. "Ah ha! Looks like somebody knows what I'm talking about." He brought his face down closer to me, unable to help gloating that he'd rattled one of us enough to betray fear. He had us now, he knew he had us, and he was enjoying the guilty strain darkening our smiles.

"Oh, he's watching you, all right," he purred, leering with an exaggerated sense of righteousness, "He sees every single time your hand goes down there and lingers a little too long, and he'll take care of you, gentlemen, just the way he took care of Onan."

ZA-BOOM!

He made a sudden loud zapping sound accompanied by the loud, sharp clap of his hands, a graphic imitation of the crackling hiss of heavenly lightning reducing some unrepentant spiller-of-seed to smoking cinders. I wasn't the only one who flinched. It was a sound that followed me all the way home.

I had good reason to be nervous about divine retribution. Although I had yet to learn how to induce orgasm, I had collected dozens of other photos since that first one, whenever I happened to stumble on an underwear ad or a beach photo or weightlifting ad or any occasion where shirts came off, where confident young men flaunted their firm, lean physiques. I hoarded all these carefully clipped-out treasures in a box I kept hidden, photos of young men with confident, trim bodies all so much nicer than mine.

I came home from that particular CCD class distraught with guilt and moral confusion. I wanted desperately to be considered good. I wanted to be a soldier of Christ. I wanted goodness to win. Suddenly all the bare male bodies in that box seemed like a roaring freight train hurtling down a track straight for disaster. I had to get off that train.

In an impulsive act I've regretted long and deeply ever since, I removed my box of treasures from its secret hiding place, started a private little fire in the downstairs fireplace, fanned the flames into life, brought my box over to the hearth, and one by one, after a last fond gaze of admiration, consigned my treasured young men to the flames.

Last to burn was my May 1943 copy of *Male Physique*.

As our Holy Confirmation approached, my mother made a terrible discovery. She was talking to her friend, Dolores, whose husband made more money than my father and whose daughters went to St George's School. Dolores let my mother know that my brother and I, as public school boys, would be *with* the St. George's students also receiving the sacrament, but we would not be included *among* them. The Catholic school students would all enter the church to receive the sacrament first, in a procession of red sacramental robes. They would be followed by the public school kids at the end of the procession wearing their best suits and neckties.

My mother was at first struck speechless. Then she quickly became furious. Her Sicilian temper was like a rapidly-spreading prairie fire, blazing ferociously and scorching everything in its path.

I came home from school to find her standing in the kitchen, her back to the window, clutching the phone to her ear and speaking to Father Cornelius in a way I'd never heard her talk before.

"Is it true? You haven't answered my question yet, Father. Are you going to shame my boys because we can't afford tuition at your expensive school?"

Father Cornelius wasn't famous for his compassion. He did nothing to change his reputation in that telephone conversation. He explained that the quality and depth of Catholic religious education placed the St George's students at a higher level of achievement than that of public school kids.

"What you mean is, you want to make sure everyone notices that my boys are not quite as rich and holy as your kids in Catholic school."

Her anger changed nothing. We ended up following them separately, in suits. But for years afterward, I remembered this entire incident incorrectly. In the confused logic of my eleven-year-old memory, the public school boys were forced to walk at the end of the procession not because they didn't go to Catholic school but because they masturbated.

Chapter 5
The Nutcracker Head Kick

I became adept at pretending. I could pass as normal, if I didn't press my luck. But there were two women who always seemed to see through my performance. All I had to do was glimpse a black Chrysler pulling up in front of our house, and my stomach muscles would knot in dread.

My mother's two best friends, the Simonetti sisters, were paying an afternoon visit. Tamara and Dolores were not Rosellas, like we were, but part of a separate but similar big Italian family clan, the Simonettis. Both women had befriended my mother when she first moved up to Seattle with her new sailor husband, when my mother didn't have any friends here in town and was stranded among critical aunts and cousins. Old Mrs Simonetti knew Nana, back when Nana and my grandfather ran a fruit and vegetable stand on Beacon Avenue. Tamara and Dolores had been kinder to the Sicilian bride from Southern California than many of my father's actual relatives, and my mother never forgot it.

They would often stop over for coffee in the afternoon, when housework was done, on the way back from the supermarket. The three of them would sit around the kitchen table playing *canasta*, and share all the news about the people they knew, who was drinking, who was cheating on his wife, who had cancer, who was betting on the horses, who was gaining weight. Though Dolores was tall and skinny, and Tamara was short and chubby, they looked like alternate versions of each other, animated Italian women doing what Italian women do best, gossiping and dissecting, bragging and giving advice.

To hear them critiquing the lives of so many others made me clench my teeth in anxiety, knowing they were very critical of me. I was sensitive to the subtlest hints of disapproval in their eyes and voices.

As always, the very sight of their approach through the kitchen window propelled me into defensive alarm. Now that we had moved to our new house, we saw them much more often. Tamara and her husband had just built a new house at exactly the same time we did, with the same contractor, just down the street from us. Both the houses went up simultaneously, just one block apart and easily in sight of each other, two comfortable brick ranch-style Fifties modern types. They had moved into theirs, with their son and two daughters, the same week we moved into ours.

One of Dolores's daughters was my brother's age. One of Tamara's daughters was my age, and that daughter, Sandra Bergamini, would quite unexpectedly evolve within the year from a tomboy with braces and a ponytail to unarguably the most beautiful girl at Maple School. None of their kids, however, were along on this particular visit. Neither were the husbands. This was just women stopping over for a couple quick hands of *canasta* and woman talk.

I watched now through the kitchen window as Tamara and Dolores closed the car doors and walked down the driveway toward the back porch.

What drew their attention to me? What elicited their probing questions and unsettling innuendos? It was my complete ignorance of what exactly it meant to be a boy. I had no clue what was socially appropriate for my gender. I was clinging to a childhood world where sex did not complicate things. No matter how hard I tried to camouflage my difference, I helplessly and constantly and blatantly deviated from expected male norms.

"Your Mom tells me you went to a ballet," said Dolores, dropping her little bomb with a smile, withholding any obvious value judgment from her voice, giving me a nice big opportunity to make them all cringe. "Did you have a good time?"

Well might she ask. "It was *The Nutcracker Suite*. It was incredible."

"Isn't it all dancing?"

"Amazing dancing."

"And you really like that?"

The smile of remembering on my face faded. I realized I'd given the wrong answer. Normal boys didn't like the ballet. They knew that I already had many marks against me. I did not participate in any sport with throwing or catching balls. I had no competitive spirit. I was bored by athletic games and never watched sports on television. I wasn't interested in cars. I wasn't interested in girls. What was worse, I wasn't smart enough to hide these deficiencies. Instead, I openly and blatantly loved opera. I memorized the lyrics to songs in musicals. I had even gone to a ballet. I loved movies and books and conversation and symphonies and art museums. Without realizing it, I was practically shouting out a declaration of homosexuality.

My defiance of the masculine code climaxed on the day I took the bus downtown and bought my very first high fidelity record. I spent an hour in the record store, and finally chose an inexpensive, discounted recording of my all-time favorite, *The Nutcracker Suite*. I had grown to love several of the most famous excerpts before finally seeing the Tchaikovsky ballet and discovering how much more there was. Now on the record jacket I saw all the names of the pieces that had been listed in the performance program. I clutched my precious purchase in both hands for the entire bus ride home.

Tamara and Dolores were sitting with my mother at the kitchen table when I got there. I blew past them with a quick hello. My brother was lying on the living room carpet in front of the television, and he got even less of an acknowledgement of his presence. I flung off my jacket, put my new purchase on our hi-fi record player, cranked up the volume in spite of my mother's guests and my brother trying to watch television, and with the first surge of music found myself transported. Without a flicker of common sense or any sane instinct of social inhibition I began leaping about the room in an ecstasy of independence and emotion.

I can't explain my silliness or insensitive timing. It was just breathless excitement with nowhere to go. I cringe now remembering that unfortunate exuberance, but I was possessed. What I was doing wasn't really ballet, it was just leaping and spinning ecstatically, arms and legs flying, and probably should never have been done anywhere near another human being.

A wild kick of pure joy connected with my brother's head. His offended wail, the blood, the bitten tongue, the panic and rage of my mother, all seem like genuine memories, just like the sound of the record being scratched as it was jerked off the turntable.

That was the launching of the family legend, to the great amusement of the Simonetti sisters, that I had kicked my brother in the head while executing ballet leaps to the "Dance of the Sugar Plum Fairy."

Need anyone say more?

Chapter 6
Bagna Calde

Many of the families in the Rosella clan and the Simonetti clan lived near each other on Beacon Hill. Often they mingled socially, bowled together, golfed together, played cards or attended meetings together at the Sons of Italy. However, between them existed an undeniable competition. The Simonettis traced their roots in Italy to the north in Tuscany. They looked down on my father, since Nana had come from a little village up in the hills near Naples. The Rosellas were considered southern or *bassa*, a lower form of Italian, the kind who smothered everything in tomato sauce. My mother was even lower as a Sicilian, which meant that she carried the taint of Africa in her blood.

Still, in spite of our family's genetic shortcomings, we were sometimes asked to join them over the holidays for special events. The one occasion I remember more than any other was the evening we were invited to share in an Italian tradition called the *bagna calde*.

The name means "hot bath" and the meal took place in the kitchen. About a dozen adults and half as many youngsters stood crowded around the kitchen table, near a pile of ripped pieces of rustic bread. Only elderly Mrs Simonetti was seated, her legs in no shape to stand for long, proud as an eagle, reigning over the banquet like a ruthless Tuscan queen. A big metal cauldron with a heating device underneath took up most of the table. It contained a bubbling lake of olive oil with other special ingredients, into which the bread bits were dipped by finger and then lifted dripping to the lips.

"Just watch how everyone else does it," said my mother, "and then you do it the same way."

Easier said than done! The *bagna calde* seemed to go against one of the most fundamental hygiene rules that my parents had imprinted into my soul. My mother could see I was distraught from my widened eyes.

I whispered, "They're double-dipping."

We had been strictly taught never to dip into a common pot with a piece of bread out of which you'd taken a bite. That was how germs were spread. This warning of germ contamination had been drilled into us. My brother and I at the dinner table would rigorously police each other against slipping into that particular sin. Here that's all everyone was doing: the entire family gathered together around the heated cauldron in the middle of the table was happily double-dipping.

"That's what *bagna calde* means," said my mother quietly to me. "It's like we're all taking a hot bath together." Seeing the question unresolved on my face, she continued, "You all eat together out of the same pot as a family, and you trust that nobody has a disease."

Sandra was like my cousin, although she was a Simonetti and I was a Rosella. Sandra and her older sister and little brother all dipped their bread in the *bagna calde* together, fearlessly risking the spread of germs. I happened to be standing next to Sandra when she turned to me, showed me her braces in a smile, and then double-dipped her bread and moved it dripping toward my lips. I was momentarily paralyzed – I could practically see her teeth marks on the bread. Then I gobbled it from her fingers, took another piece of bread from the pile, dipped, munched, double-dipped and offered it to her.

It was the beginning of a friendship.

That first summer, when I had only one friend, I spent many afternoons at the Bergaminis, learning how to play card games with Sandra. We grew to trust each other and shared a few secrets. She told me the name of the one boy she liked, the only one. Now I remember back to her confession and shake my head in wonder. He was the man she married.

But no one then knew a thing about any such boy who was lucky enough to be favored by Sandra. According to popular opinion, Sandra Bergamini didn't notice boys, like she saw right through them. Now she was just considered a tom boy, outdoing boys whenever she could. Soon she would become known as the Ice Queen, beautiful but untouchable. Her beauty had yet to claim her.

Back when I first got to know her, when we shared bread at the *bagne calde*, Sandra had looked more like a geeky boy. She wore braces on her teeth and her hair was pulled tightly back from her scalp in a rigorous ponytail. No one expected her to turn into a beauty. We clowned around, roughhoused and thought nothing of it. We were knockabout friends before her beauty happened to her, before the braces came off and her hair came down.

    She trusted me in fourth grade when we were the new kids in the neighborhood, so we managed to stay friends when she changed and all the boys at Maple Elementary School suddenly wanted desperately to know her and I was the lucky one who did.

PART TWO

Chapter 7
The War of the Worlds

Nana ended up in a nursing home.

She had become disoriented and lost downtown, unable to find the right bus home. She waited at the wrong bus stops. She was mugged. Her purse was snatched. She kept losing things. She fell down the back stairs. She had bruises and scabs on her legs. My father visited her every morning and every evening. One morning he found her in the basement, at the bottom of the stairs, where she had lain all night. He had no choice. She begged not to go to the nursing home. Twice she packed her suitcase and tried to escape.

I mention her because forty years before that, after her beloved husband's early death, she used to take the bus daily across the city to the Catholic cemetery where he was buried. She would throw herself on his grave and beg God to take her, too. She made that journey every single morning for seven years. He meant more to her than anyone else in her life, but at the nursing home when we showed Nana her own wedding picture, she pointed at the handsome bridegroom standing beside her and asked, "Who is that man?"

Memories are one of life's great disappointments.

We act like these fragile treasures left over from our experiences are ours forever. If only they were! Unfortunately, the images fade, they get jumbled into the wrong order, we lose some of them to time, others are misplaced and still others disintegrate utterly.

How often we say we'll never forget. How often we do.

What a cheat that we can't keep them. They're just flickers, and gone. And the older you get, the harder it is to remember what really happened to you. We remember what justifies us, what comforts us, the parts that fit together easily, the parts that seem to make sense. We modify the past so that it fits what we think of ourselves. We leave out whatever makes us uncomfortable, whatever we can't understand.

With that qualification, what comes next is a memory of remembering a memory. I'm about ten years old, it's a rainy Seattle evening, I'm downtown alone and at this age I don't usually go downtown alone, much less after dark. The entire context of the memory is lost. It's floating free, like a dream. For some reason, on my way to the bus stop, I'm passing Woolworth's and before I know what I'm doing, I've glanced at my watch, confirmed that I've got fifteen minutes before my bus arrives, and pushed open the door, to be hit in the face by the buttery heat of freshly popped popcorn.

I know that smell. I've been here before.

While we were still living next door, Nana would frequently take my brother and me downtown on the bus, where we would see a matinee in one of the grand old theaters that used to cluster at the intersection of Fifth and Pike, at the Coliseum or the Blue Mouse or the Music Box, and then afterward we would often stop by her favorite little independent restaurant, a spick-and-span, brightly-lit hole in the wall called the Home of the Green Apple Pie. Its name was ironic for us, because the reason we went there was to enjoy their *other* pie specialty, which was wild blackberry. They used real wild blackberries in their pies, Nana assured us, the smaller, authentic, native berry. Wild blackberry pie was one of Nana's own specialties. Only the Home of the Green Apple Pie made them up to her standards.

Since the restaurant was so close to Woolworth's, we had frequently ended up browsing through the million and one things you could find in a store like that. To my delight, I had discovered a tiny book department, which is where I'm heading now, as I make my wet way over the wooden floorboards. It's merely a couple shelves, really, and a single shelf featuring the charming, inexpensive set of little hardbound volumes called the Looking Glass Library.

How often I used to come here with Nana! Making sure not to get the books wet from my rainy jacket, I glance over the titles. I already have *Five Children and It* by Edith Nesbitt. I already have *The Haunted Library*, a terrifying collection of ghost stories. I already have *The Princess and the Goblin*, one of the greatest fairy tales ever written.

But what about this one? This purple volume?

I slide it out and look at the cover. *The War of the Worlds* by H. G. Wells. Giant tripods roaming over a desolate landscape. I turn the book over. Little people on fire. In the distance, a city is in flames. Another tripod appears to be coming straight toward me.

That does it. Somehow I already know this story. The memory comes roaring back at me. As I stand there dripping on the wooden floor of the tiny book department, I remember my first introduction to Wells' nightmarish tale of alien invasion.

As a child, I received comic books through the mail as a gift from a friend of my mother's who supplemented her income by selling magazine subscriptions. Mrs Winterburn already made sure that we received the current issue every month of *Modern Screen*, which the whole family treated as a factual news magazine and read each issue religiously.

But when I turned seven, and my younger brother was nearly five, Mrs Winterburn began sending my brother and me each a subscription to comic books. The first year she sent me *Uncle Scrooge*, and the second year *Tarzan*. But nothing prepared me for the third year.

Suddenly I begin receiving a line of comic books I went on to collect and treasure for years afterward, the series of gorgeous, sophisticated *Classics Illustrated*. Not only did their lively retellings arouse my curiosity to read some of the greatest novels ever written, but they included one comic book in particular, a terrifying adaptation of a science fiction novel I'd never heard of before by an author named H. G. Wells.

The alarming cover grabbed my attention. The upsetting story gave me nightmares. I can only look back and ponder that comic book's enormous impact on my life. Wells' tale of ruthless colonization from Mars caused a seismic rupture in my thinking. The cover alone of the *War of the Worlds* comic was shiver-inducing, with towering tripods shooting their death-ray at three human soldiers who don't stand a chance. It excited and horrified me. I read the comic over and over again, memorizing every panel.

Then forgot all about it in the ongoing sensory assault of childhood, until this dark and rainy afternoon when fate and coincidence have nudged me into over-bright, over-heated Woolworth's so I can go one step farther.

I seized the small purple book with the title of my all-time favorite comic, and rushed to the cashier. I could hardly keep it in its paper bag on the bus ride home. The moment I got it in my house, I retreated downstairs to the recreation room in the basement, turned off all the lights except for one small lamp, so that no one would find me and interrupt my reading.

Hours later, by the time my mother called me upstairs for dinner, I could no longer hear her. My ears were ringing with the terrified cries of "The Martians are coming! the Martians are coming!" I had forgotten all about hunger, all about eating, hardly remembered what dinner even was. I was witnessing the streets jammed with desperate, stampeding people in the great evacuation of London.

"Dinner is ready! You get up here this minute."

I tried to continue reading at the kitchen table with the book in my lap. My mother was not amused.

"Close that book this minute."

I did so. The moment I had forced down the last sprig of broccoli, I retreated to the basement, and had to be called back upstairs twice.

"It's your turn to wash the dishes. Don't make me call you again."

Though I took my usual place stretched out on the living room carpet with the family in the evening, I was only pretending to watch television, until finally my exasperated mother said, "If you're going to read, why don't you go where there's better light."

I didn't have to be told twice. I tucked my bookmark in place, scrambled to my feet, and bolted downstairs.

When I had turned the last page, I lay there stretched out on the sofa stunned and grateful and exhilarated and emotionally drained. Earth was saved. But just barely.

I went back upstairs and re-joined the family watching *Gunsmoke*, sliding unnoticed into my usual place on the carpet during the climactic shootout. During the commercial break I made the mistake of commenting on what a great book I had just finished reading.

"Finished?" said my mother. "Not the book you just bought today? Already? It only lasted you one day?"

My father shook his head in disappointment, his eyes remaining focused on the television screen, as though expecting at any moment to be given some vital information about toothpaste or deodorant. "Use your head before you waste your money," he said. As a man who worked a fifteen-hour day, he knew only too well what money was worth.

"What are libraries for?" asked my mother. "You spend all your money on books, you read them in a day, and then where are you? What's the use of a book after you've read it? You put it on the shelf. It gathers dust."

But no sensible reasoning could reach me.

Chapter 8
Too Many Books

The older you grow, the more you watch addictions happen to the people around you. Not just cigarettes and alcohol and heroin, but sex and sale-shopping and watching television, any compulsive, repeatable behavior that results in a taste of happiness. Little habits turn into obsessions. We all want so desperately to inject joy into our daily lives.

My mother and father were sensible, hard-working people and didn't have habits. As they quietly struggled to make ends meet, making sure their two sons never had to worry about money, how discouraged they must have been to notice in their eldest son the beginning of a dangerous and expensive habit that would make him a poor man for the rest of his life.

Their son was falling in love with books.

It began with *Rinkitink in Oz*, the very first book I ever owned. It was passed on to me by a cousin who had outgrown it, in a box of books she no longer wanted. The other titles have faded away, but not *Rinkitink*. I read it over and over again. Ownership made the story more special than reading it in a library book. For years it has been my treasured loadstone of book love, my most valuable possession, shown only to the few whom I knew would handle it with respect. The adventures of the fat, funny king and his friendship with the handsome young prince completely captivated me. Now I can't help but read it through entirely different eyes.

Seeing that I had fallen in love with Oz, my mother's sister in California gave me *The Land of Oz*, the powerful second book in the Oz series. Aunt Lorraine had no idea that the book's bold climax is one of the most upsetting endings in children's literature. After spending most of the story with the boy Tip and his entourage of unusual friends seeking to rescue the captured Princess Ozma, young readers discover in the final pages that the witch Mombi has concealed the princess in the one place she could be sure they would never look – the princess has been changed into the boy Tip himself. The story ends with Tip vanishing as he turns back into the princess, opening up the hideous possibility that I might also harbor a princess hiding inside me.

The terror of being a girl in disguise, like that of being an alien from outer space, was smothered, buried, denied and purposely forgotten.

Books became what my allowance was for. I discovered that the Bon Marche downtown had a book department where they carried all the Oz books in a handsome hardcover set. The very first book I bought with my own money was the third book in the series, *Ozma of Oz*, with its sexy, dramatic cover portrait of a far-from-childish Ozma. When my mother glanced over at the living room sofa and saw that I'd finished it, she threw up her hands in exasperation.

"Already? Use some common sense! You wasted two dollars and fifty cents on a book you read in a day!"

Soon, because I carried a book with me everywhere I went, because my glasses were always sliding down my nose, I was nicknamed "the Professor." Oblivious to sarcasm and connotations, I never went anywhere without a book. It was my guarantee that life wouldn't bore me.

I discovered Walden Books downtown, and soon I knew exactly which bus to catch to get there. My bedside collection of books doubled and then quadrupled, filling up all the little bookshelves on my side of the bedroom, then growing up in piles like mushrooms around my bed. The joy I felt in my growing library was frustrated by the bedroom's single large window, which was just above my bed on my side of the room and took up a huge chunk of available space. Every other bit of wall was taken up with books, and when I ran out of wall, I began piling.

My habit was out of control.

After a Saturday afternoon trying to vacuum the carpet in the bedroom, bumping into the piles of books, tripping over them while trying to vacuum the carpet, my mother finally turned off the vacuum and summoned me to the bedroom with a shout.

"There are too many books in here," she complained, when I appeared scared and breathless in the doorway, fearing her no-nonsense tone of voice, my finger in whatever book I was reading substituting for the bookmark I had been in too much of a hurry to find. "How am I supposed to vacuum in here? There's not enough room to turn around!" In demonstrating how crowded it was, my mother inadvertently caused the cord to the vacuum cleaner to knock over a pile of paperbacks behind her.

"Be careful!" I cried, and dropped to my knees, desperately hoping that none of the corners were bent. I kept my books in perfect condition.

She was unrepentant. "I have to be able to clean in this bedroom," she ordained. "Now I want you to pick up all these books off the floor and put them where they belong. No more piling books around the bed."

"But where can they go?"

"They need to go on the shelves."

"But there's no more room."

"Make room. They are not going on the floor. Maybe it's time to get rid of some of them."

"No!" I wailed.

The easy solution quickly presented itself. My brother's side of the bedroom had no such window. My brother owned a total of nine books, all of them gifts. Exchanging sides of the bedroom was the obvious and effortless way to solve the bookshelving crisis.

To everyone's surprise, my brother emphatically refused to change sides of the bedroom with me. Why? He had no good reason, he just insisted that he wanted to stay right where he was. It was a dreadful blockade to hit, because there was only one other choice left if I wanted to keep my book collection all in the same room with me.

Down in the basement there was a spare bedroom.

Moving downstairs by myself was the last thing I wanted to do. Everyone else in the family slept on the main floor. I'd be alone down there. The bedroom was right next to the creepiest room in the house, the small, dark wine cellar, with its barrels of homemade wine, its sour vinegar smell, its single dangling light bulb, its spiders and its mice.

But the only place I could keep all my books together was down there. They didn't fit anywhere else.

I went downstairs and sat in the room. Maybe the privacy would be nice. Until now the room had been filled with old furniture, an unused desk, an extra bed, closet space for clothes no one wore anymore but weren't quite ready to give to the Goodwill. It was stuffy and overcrowded, a place you put things you didn't want to think about.

If my books had to move, then I would have to move with them.

That night at the dinner table I grimly announced my decision. Was my brother delighted to discover he'd have the whole bedroom to himself? Was he frightened to realize he'd be spending the nights alone from now on? We were both far too young, of course, to realize that things would never be the same between us again, that all our trusting whispers during the night had come to an end.

I cleared out the spare bedroom. I bought more Erect-a-Shelf and built bookshelves all around the room. I sorted and divided up my books by author and topic, science fiction over here, classics over there, novels front and center, Shakespeare on this shelf, Arabian Nights on that shelf. I created an upper bookshelf in the sliding-door closets, above the hanging clothes. There I lined up my treasures, my Oz books, my collection of Jules Verne.

The huge roll-top desk became my treasure vault. I found a use for every single cubbyhole. What felt like exile at first quickly changed into an exhilarating freedom. It was a secret twilight kingdom underneath the rest of the family, and it was mine. I had my own downstairs bathroom. I loved the much-bigger bed. I had twice as much closet space. And what a peaceful place to study! I couldn't hear the television down there. I was a naturally happy student who genuinely enjoyed studying, and now I had the perfect arrangement for studying and reading. My exile had created my own private library in the depths of the house.

Chapter 9
The Haunted Staircase

  I immersed myself in book after book, reading away my afternoons and evenings, hiding out in my secluded bunker in the basement, living anyone else's life but my own. Encouraged by David Starr's attractive matching sets of small magazines that lined his bedroom, I started reading science fiction magazines like *Amazing* and *Fantastic Stories*, and discovered the intoxicating delight of Ace Double Novels, where the story only goes half-way through, and then you flip over the paperback for a whole different science fiction cover and story on the other side.

  My escape into books down in the privacy of the basement was daily and sacred. After school it was my sanctuary. No one else spent time down there. Just opening the basement door was refreshing – cooler air came whooshing up through the open doorway. As soon as I closed the door behind me, I could stop pretending and be completely myself. The carpeted stairs led down into a dimly lit, hushed private domain where only my mother occasionally intruded to put a load of laundry in the washing machine.

  Whether I was sitting at my roll-top desk or reading in bed or curled up on the sofa in the recreation room, I would keep the light low and focused, the rest of the basement in darkness, to protect my private little reading world against being invaded by another member of the family. My brother had begun to watch more television, and with the shows my parents enjoyed, the set was on most of the time. The mindless assault of commercials and canned laughter rang in our ears all day long. At last I had a sanctuary where those singsong words and fake applause were muffled by the intervening floor. The chants were deflected, the jingles blunted. Getting lost in books downstairs became my way to escape.

Generally this was only interrupted by family meals and school obligations, but occasionally on the weekend, depending on the holiday and the season, there would be one of those big mandatory family gatherings at Nana's house. These punctuated my childhood, ruining whatever weekend they fell on, where I was forced to wear good clothes and expected to behave all day long – these events were never short – and where I admittedly took out my frustration at being exiled from my books in the sadistic delight of terrorizing my cousins by telling scary stories.

Why I ever took to making up such stories I don't remember. Possibly my own vulnerability to attacks of fear led me to enjoy inventing them and inducing fear in others. When trapped after a huge dinner in a house full of family members, deprived of my books, with the men settling in the living room to watch football on television and the women gossiping in the kitchen washing dishes, stranded with my cousins with nothing to do, telling grim urban legends passed the time and provided a wicked outlet for my pent-up anxieties. My stories were as frightening as I could make them. I simply got too good at it. My mother received several angry phone calls from my aunts, complaining that my terrible stories were giving their children sleepless nights.

Of course, that only encouraged me.

I remember a holiday gathering – was it Easter or Christmas? I can no longer recall – when I led Linda and Nina and little Anita, three of my more gullible cousins, into the narrow staircase closet in the middle of my grandmother's house that led up to the unused bedrooms on the second floor. While the adults watched television and washed the dishes, we sat crouched close together, knees to knees on the stairs, my brother and my cousins, and as usual they demanded that I tell them a story.

Or at least that's how I remember it.

"Well, you probably already know about the tenant who used to live upstairs here at Nana's?" I asked, turning off the staircase light, gesturing up toward one of the dark rooms on the landing above us. "I think it was that one, on that side. I don't have to make that story up, because it's true. You know what happened to him, right?"

Almost as a chorus they uniformly admitted they didn't.

Of course, they didn't. He hadn't existed until a moment ago. "Well, you know he died right here in this staircase, don't you?"

"Stop it, Nicky, don't tell anymore," interrupted Nina, in a panic. "That's enough, no more."

But now I was warming to my subject. "No, really, it's not a scary story, it's the truth. He fell down these stairs. Didn't your Mom ever tell you that? Broke his neck at the bottom. Nana was the one who found him."

"Come on, you're making this up."

"No, really," I said in my most sincere voice. "Ask Nana, if you don't believe me. I thought everyone knew how he died. That night she had just baked one of her wild blackberry pies…"

"Just like tonight," Linda chirped in anticipation. Nana's wild blackberry pie was a holiday staple, and everyone's favorite dessert.

"Yeah, just like tonight. Well, that night, in order for the pie to cool, Nana put it here in the staircase. No one knows exactly what happened, but the poor guy was coming down the stairs and he must not have seen the pie there until too late. Obviously he tried to avoid stepping on it. He must have lost his balance, fell down the last steps, and hit his neck on the edge of a stair."

No one budged.

"What happened to the pie?" whispered Nina.

"Untouched. But after that no one wanted to eat it. Nana had to throw it out."

They were so quiet I could hear them breathing.

"Six months later," I went on, in an even softer voice, "we were all here at Nana's house for dinner."

"How come we weren't here?" objected Anita.

"It wasn't a big dinner, it was just a little dinner for my father's birthday, and Nana had another wild blackberry pie cooling here in the staircase. Right there where you're sitting, Nina, that's where she put it because it was still a little too hot and it's so nice and cool in here."

Nina looked thoroughly uncomfortable.

"We were all sitting down eating dinner when suddenly this terrible sound thunders through the whole house. Boom! Boomboomboom! It sounded like something heavy falling down the stairs. But everyone was seated at the dinner table. My father ran to the staircase door, and flung it open.

"No one was in the staircase – but right there where you're sitting – all over the stairs was smashed wild blackberry pie."

Linda and Nina both screamed. Anita burst into tears. They scrambled to their feet and banged open the staircase door, rushing into the kitchen to throw their arms around their mother.

"Nicky told us another scary story!" they wailed.

Chapter 10
Donovan's Brain

It wasn't the first time I got in trouble for telling horror stories to my cousins. Wherever we happened to be, whatever relative's house we were at, I would find a suitable place away from the adults where I could turn down the lights, a basement or bedroom or guest room full of coats, gather them together, hush them up, set the mood, lower my voice, make it all sound very realistic, and then scare them out of their wits.

But the real, secret truth was that the biggest coward of them all was me.

As long as I was telling the story, I was smart enough not to fear any of it, knowing the whole thing was all tricks and whistles – but when the storytelling was taken out of my hands, when I didn't know what was going to happen next, my anxiety would rocket out of control and I would become a whimpering chicken. What I dreaded was going to happen became as real for me as what actually did. My fears outsoared reality. I saw possibilities for disaster lurking in wait everywhere for just about everyone. I became known in the family for jumps and whimpers and shouts, for abruptly fleeing scary television shows, for leaping for cover behind armchairs and sofas and peering out from behind them toward the television screen, afraid to witness the occurrence of my worst fears.

I watched the first hour of *The Thing* on our tiny black-and-white television screen from all the way across the living room, cowering in the kitchen doorway. Frequently my cries and leaps and flinches scared the people around me more than the movie. One of my jerk-aways caused my mother to spill her coffee. In exasperation, she forced me to leave the room. Aunts and uncles were warned that I was not allowed to watch anything scary on television when visiting.

In spite of parental vigilance, a scary movie would occasionally manage to slip through. At a Saturday morning matinee at the old Beacon Theatre, along with the main feature of *Francis the Talking Mule* they showed the preview to the next movie coming to the Beacon, *The Creature from the Black Lagoon*. The trailer was enough. I was beside myself. Until then I had always enjoyed swimming. The very idea of being grabbed from below!

I had to have both my mother and grandmother saying the rosary with me that night, one on either side of my bed. What if a creature like that reached up and snagged me – especially if I was just wearing my bathing suit?

But the movie that cemented my reputation as traumatically impressionable was the science fiction thriller, *Donovan's Brain*.

I watched it alone in a dark living room at my Aunt Lorraine's house in Long Beach. My brother and cousins were riding bicycles down in the flood control, being cooked alive by the California sun. The adults were drinking lemonade and beer in the back yard, in lounge chairs beneath the lemon trees. No one noticed that I had slipped off alone.

I was switching through the channels looking for cartoons when I fatefully stumbled on the movie. It was halfway over, and at first I thought it was about some kind of prehistoric fish in an aquarium until I realized that it was a human brain. I kept my hand on the knob, trying to change the channel. I couldn't make myself do it.

I watched in mounting panic.

Suspended alive in a big fish tank, surviving the loss of his body in a plane crash, Donovan's brain has enormous psychic powers and begins controlling the scientists keeping it alive. At a very tense moment, one of the heroes grabs a gun and rushes into the room, aiming at the brain in the tank and determined to destroy it. But not fast enough. The brain takes control of the scientist, and the gun he has pointed at the brain slowly, slowly, slowly turns around until it's pointing right at his own head.

Blam! The scientist shoots himself between the eyes.

With a yelp and a wail, I leaped for cover behind the sofa. That's where my mother and aunt found me when they came running in from the patio.

"What happened? What happened?"

"Are you hurt?"

My mother took one glance at the television screen, realized what had happened, and snapped it off with a click.

"What's this? What are you watching?" She had no sympathy for my tears. They were the tears of the guilty. "You know better than to watch this kind of crap. What are the rules?"

I knew the rules, all right, but it was too late. I'd been caught watching scary movies again. There would be no sleep for me that night without rosary beads and company, my previous collection of childhood terrors now featuring something new to be afraid of, the creeping fear that someone's brain might choose to control me.

Chapter 11
The Bookmobile

My fourth grade year at Maple School came and went. I don't remember a single one of my experiences as a new kid. I appear to have floated through it. Who was my teacher? Did I have any friends? I suspect I was just oblivious to the whole human whirlpool around me, content to do nothing but read away my afternoons as soon as I got home from school, plowing through one book after another.

I appear to have now and then spent a couple hours with David Starr, but I don't remember us doing much more than play Scrabble and hang out together reading science fiction paperbacks or comics up in his bedroom. Most of the time, as soon as the bell rang at the end of the school day, I'd walk straight through the after-school games on the playfield and quickly hike the two blocks home, where I would disappear downstairs until dinner.

Only one haunting memory remains.

Although Maple School did have its own library, presided over by the authoritarian Mrs Hayes, it was quite small, budget-constricted, and stocked mostly with picture books for younger children, with a little non-fiction intended primarily to amplify topics in the classroom. But we had one other source of books. On the first Tuesday of every month, our classroom schedule would be arranged to accommodate the arrival of the Bookmobile.

Maybe it belonged to Seattle Public Schools. Maybe it came from Seattle Public Library. It was a reclaimed bus turned library on wheels that drove onto the playground with a merrily honking horn. That sound would cause everyone in class to rise to their feet in a sudden scramble, straining to see out the windows. Denise Hobbs, the librarian behind the steering wheel, would wave like a celebrity in a parade, give a hearty laugh, and then park next to the main school building, open both doors, and lower both sets of stairs.

One classroom full of students at a time would get to visit the Bookmobile, going through it in groups of five because there was so little space inside, in one door and out the other. Denise would check in the books being returned from last month, and then help each student find a book or two within their reach and interest to check out for the month to come.

That anyone could do this for a whole school now fills me with awe. At the time, I only knew that I could hardly wait for my turn to go down that narrow aisle between books on either side, with Denise sitting at the fold-out desk at the front. She was a skinny little thing, not much taller than I was, with a booming laugh that seemed to jiggle the bus. The distinctive thing about her was her hair, so fine and thin and blond that it fluttered about her head more like a mist, insubstantial, a feathery chaos that looked like it was about to blow away.

"I'll bet you've never read *Treasure Island*, have you?"

I shook my head, and took the book into my hands. It would become one of my favorite books of all time.

"Have you read *The Black Stallion* yet? Some people really love it."

I went on to read *The Black Stallion Returns* and then *The Black Stallion Revolts* and then…

You could check out three books for the month, and I always checked out as many books as I could. I would happily descend the little attached steps on the side of the bus with my treasures in my arms.

The main memory I have was of the month our room got to go first. That's when the selection in the Bookmobile hasn't been picked over yet. How full the shelves were! Denise recognized me with a smile, and helped me select three good ones. I climbed down out of the Bookmobile in bliss. Most of the rest of the day, instead of whatever I should have been doing, I spent reading my newly checked-out books, and as the day began drawing to a close realized in dismay I'd finished two of them. I had only one skinny book left unread, and was facing a month before her next visit.

Desperation breeds rash behavior. As a boy who always obeyed the rules, I found myself frantic at the thought of running out of books. I watched out the window of my fourth grade classroom as the pupils from each room at Maple School lined up outside the bus and went through, and when the last class had exited the Bookmobile with their month's selection, I remember asking for a hall pass and instead of walking straight down the hall to the boys' room, continuing past my destination and out the side door of the building, where it was only a dozen steps to the parked bus. The door was still open, and before anyone could see me, I climbed back up into the Bookmobile.

"My goodness!" said Denise, looking up as I came down the aisle. "And here I thought I was all done for the day." She took another closer look at me. "Do you have a twin brother? Someone who looked a lot like you just went through here and checked out *Danny Dunn and the Anti-Gravity Paint*."

"It was me," I confirmed enthusiastically, delighted that she remembered. "I loved it!"

"You've already finished it?" She was amused. "I'll make sure to bring more *Danny Dunn* books next month. But didn't you also check out *Visit to the Mushroom Planet*?"

"I loved that one, too!" I confirmed. Only now do I find it amazing that out of a school full of children, she seemed to always remember exactly what she'd given you. At that point, I held the books out to her. "I was hoping to return them and check out some others."

"What have you been doing?" exclaimed Denise. "Reading all day? I can see I've got a regular little bookworm on my hands."

My guilty smile made her laugh. She had a loud laugh that felt too big for the tight confines of the bus. She didn't have much left to offer me. By the end of the day, all the classes at Maple School had gone through the bus and made their selections. The shelves were nearly empty. "It's pretty much picked over, but we should be able to find something," said Denise, scowling at the shelves and running her finger over the titles on the spines.

I ended up going home with a couple more *Freddy the Pig* books I hadn't read yet. When the Bookmobile drove away that day, honking, I got the feeling Denise Hobbs could see right through the windows into the classroom and was waving just at me. From that day onward, she would save a couple of her favorite books for me up at the front of the Bookmobile, set aside under my name, and she would always make me tell her my thoughts on the books I was returning. I took this assignment very seriously. I would plan my book reports to her for days in advance.

Thanks to that loud-laughing, horn-honking librarian, I always hurried home on Bookmobile day with my arms full of unread books, oblivious to the afternoon sunshine, oblivious to the shouts and laughter of the other kids on the playfield, blind to the buds on the trees, deaf to the birds eagerly welcoming spring breezes, to give my mother a quick hello, fling open the basement door and escape from the world down into the cool depths of my underground hideaway, a contented little loner only occasionally struck by my own numbing solitude.

Chapter 12
Gabby

Gabriel Salvaggio was a young New Jersey construction worker, lean and bow-legged and full of himself in a delightfully comic Italian-American manner. He was in his mid-twenties, and not exactly good-looking, but attractive in a cocky, strutting way. He was full of personality and good nature, always eager to tell a joke, always ready to do a favor for a friend, all the time knowing perfectly well that when he wanted to be charming, he was irresistible.

He didn't go to college. As soon as he escaped from high school, Gabby had started working up and down the east coast. He'd lost his last job, and was looking for work. His mother's sister had settled in the Pacific Northwest, and so shortly after Christmas, when the east coast was snowbound, he packed up his few belongings and headed for Seattle, where he took over renting his Aunt Tessie's basement which he rigged up as an impromptu bachelor pad.

He entered our lives when one of the line workers at my father's vegetable packing plant decided to return to Greece, and my father found out that Tessie Albanese's nephew was looking for work. Gabby started working for my father down on Western Avenue in the produce-packaging warehouse, and because he was strong and smart, he was soon driving the forklift and loading trucks. No one could have worked with my father for long without being drawn into one of his passionate conversations about baseball and in particular the Seattle Rainiers, whom he went to see play in Sick's Stadium at least once a year. When he discovered that Gabby had played shortstop in the semi-pro leagues back east, he promptly started planting in Gabby's mind the idea of being the coach for my brother's Little League team.

The team had lost their coach. The garrulous old coot who had coached the Veterans of Foreign Wars team for the last ten years had suffered a stroke. Though he insisted he was fully recovered, his wife had proclaimed, "I'm not ready to be a widow yet," and he had sheepishly resigned from coaching. Tryouts for the Little League season had scarcely begun. The VFW team desperately needed someone at the helm, or it would have to be dropped from the league roster.

I remember the night we had Gabby over to the house for dinner. Mom got out the best table cloth and the best silver, and we ate in the dining room instead of as usual in the kitchen. She cooked his favorite dishes, *manicotti* and *polenta*. In a matter of minutes his expansive personality took over the table. He was a complete entertainer, telling wild tale after tale of his adventures while roofing in Boston or painting warehouses in D.C. while he chewed with gusto and cleaned his plate several times.

I was spellbound by him. Gabby possessed all the masculine self-confidence anyone needed to saunter through life, and I was exactly the opposite, convinced I was a masculine fraud, doing my best to imitate guys who were really guys. Where I had a soft and flabby body, Gabby was broad-shouldered and trim, a natural athlete. He threw a baseball as though that was the specific activity the human arm had been designed for, casual and effortless, the way you might clear your throat or blow your nose.

He and my brother went out into the backyard after dinner and threw a baseball back and forth. My Dad watered the lawn. My Mom washed the dishes. I watched jealously from the kitchen window.

"Go out and join them," said my mother, glancing in my direction as she rinsed off a plate, easily seeing how left out I felt. "Get your glove and go out there."

I never would have dared.

"How are you ever going to learn how to throw a ball if you don't do it?"

I had no answer for my mother. Couldn't she see how humiliating it would be to slow down and ruin their enjoyment with my poor throwing skills? I couldn't bear the shame of forcing myself on two athletes.

My pride, huge and invisible, blocked me from revealing to our attractive guest my embarrassing athletic deficiencies. My brother and Gabby would, of course, kindly have let me join them throwing the ball back and forth, but they would have tolerated my intrusion in silent frustration. They would be forced to politely, patiently suffer my inadequacies hoping that I would soon get tired or lose interest.

"I've got homework." It was lame, but the best excuse I could muster. I flung open the basement door and closed it behind me, cutting off sight and sound of the athletic duo performing in the back yard, turning off the staircase light and closing my bedroom door behind me, determined not to come back upstairs and say goodbye.

What started out as a scorching hot day had managed to cloud over while we had dinner, and it wasn't long before the first fat drops of rain began pelting the window-well of my basement sanctuary. Sliding my bookmark into place, without turning the basement light back on, I tiptoed up the stairs and stood on the top step, my hand on the doorknob. I didn't open the door. I stood there, listening.

I heard Mom call out the kitchen door, "Aren't you boys getting a little wet out there?"

"No, Mom," my brother insisted. "It's hardly raining."

"Raining?" I heard my father in the kitchen now. "Shit, it wasn't supposed to rain today." My father seldom swore. He had chosen today, after three days of sunny weather, to paint the patio table with finish. It was drying in the patio. "The rain is going to ruin it."

Effortlessly Gabby took charge of the situation. "Do you mind if your car gets a little wet?" he asked from the kitchen doorway. Judging from the proximity of his voice, he and my brother had finally surrendered to the increasing rainfall. "Move it out onto the driveway, and we'll put the table in the garage."

The screen door slammed, the door closed, and I heard the car starting up outside. Standing in the darkness at the top of the basement stairs, I could hear the rain pattering on the roof and gargling down the gutter pipes, and then Gabby shouting something outside and my father shouting back. I became too curious to sulk any longer, flung open the door, and took two steps into the kitchen.

The sky had grown dark. The rain was coming down in hot, angry sheets. I was just in time to see, through the kitchen window, my father backing the car out of the driveway at the same time that Gabby lifted up the patio table all by himself, a feat that usually took two of us, one at either end, and carrying it on his back like a turtle with a wooden shell single-handedly walked it into the vacated garage and out of the rain.

The freshly-finished table was saved.

What I remember was Gabby coming back inside, the hero of the hour but completely drenched, his shirt sopping. My father hurriedly offered him a dry shirt of his own and suddenly, without warning, as though my wildest secret wish had been granted, Gabby peeled off his sopping shirt over his head.

His body was smooth and tight and flat as a plank. Fully aware that he was easy on the eyes, he self-consciously enjoyed the family's admiration before he pulled on my father's dry shirt. I was breathless, trying to imagine that kind of physical confidence. I may have stared too long. He noticed, and gave me a wink.

Gabby took the job as coach. The Veterans of Foreign Wars had never signed up such a popular coach, or had such a big turnout for their team. One try-out session was all it took for him to see how poor I was at throwing and catching and hitting the ball. And how good my brother was. He was named one of the starting line-up.

Something magic happened and steadily grew between my brother and Gabby. He brought out the best in my brother, honed his throwing and hitting skills, polished his natural strengths and brought out new ones, and we all watched him get better and better. Strangers cheered for my brother in the stands and called him by name as though they knew him. He became the VFW star player.

I didn't make the team.

Chapter 13
The Baseball Solution

My parents were thrilled that my brother was such a natural athlete. Other Little League parents were constantly complimenting them on my brother's spectacular catch or effortless home run. Mom and Dad would glow with pride. They were more than ready to commit many evenings a week to volunteering for Little League, transporting kids to and from various practice fields, supervising skill drills, organizing snacks.

There was only one problem: me.

Naturally they didn't want to leave me home alone during ball practice, the only member of the family who wasn't included. But the sad truth was that I very much was *not* included, that I didn't share the passion that bonded the three of them, and that was an irrefutable fact.

I was not a baseball player.

I was a bookworm.

In a family with athletic values, an anomaly had occurred. I had no athletic virtues. Not by any stretch of the imagination was I good enough to be a member of the team.

Under the circumstances, Gabby had shrugged his shoulders helplessly and made an out-in-left-field suggestion that could possibly solve the problem.

"It's just a thought."

It was more than a thought. It was a solution, of sorts, and so my parents approved it, and authorized Gabby to make the offer to me.

"Well, I suppose you're not totally surprised that you didn't make the team," he began, with his usual charming lack of tact. "But I'd sorta like to include you, and I did have one idea…"

It was the best compromise they could arrive at, and though it might possibly stunt my self-esteem, at least it included me. It was the only arrangement possible that was fair to the other boys and still gave me a role and allowed our family to participate as a family.

"And will I get a uniform?"

"You bet," said Gabby.

I was offered the one position left open that would still guarantee me a VFW uniform and allow me to travel everywhere with the team.

I could be the batboy.

In this case, a batboy who was also older and bigger and weighed more than many boys on the actual team, a pudgy, short-waisted boy who, considering his size, might look poured into his tight uniform shirt, not to mention being clumsy, self-conscious, and completely lacking in athletic prowess.

I agreed to it.

I would come to every practice and every game and serve the other boys, the athletes, the real young men. I would tote the bats, the balls and the gear, and pick up after them, and cheer them on. I basically accepted my athletic shortcomings, hiding my embarrassment, trying to enjoy the camaraderie of being on a team with other boys.

The season began. We played our first games. Desperately hiding my boredom, I tried to stay interested, tried to keep my attention focused on that profoundly uninteresting ball, tried to remember to pick up the bats and headgear wherever they were flung.

Baseball practice cut hugely into my morale, as well as into my reading time. After a long afternoon following the players through their interminable practices and games, when I finally got home I made quick work of dinner and wasted no time dashing downstairs, closing the basement door behind me. I would barricade myself into my room with just one light over my shoulder, reading hungrily, gulping it down in desperate doses. Books were the only place I could hide and heal.

I was reading less. I was healing less.

Only once did I fall apart with shame and regret. It was triggered by simple, childish name-calling, and a nasty little phrase that had taunted me more than once. For some reason, it stung me that afternoon.

Two cocky young guys on the team were playing catch on the upper playfield as I crossed it on the way home. One of them, Louie Bianchi, had an unbuttoned shirt that blew open as he threw and caught the ball, flapping around his tight young body, supple and defined and just about perfect, showing off in an act of bravado that was far beyond me.

When he saw me looking in his direction, he called out to me, "Hey, fat boy – oops, I mean batboy!" It was a tired joke that I had learned to endure and ignore. But that day, coming from succulent, mean-spirited Louie Bianchi, it sliced right into me.

I came home shaking and frustrated and on the edge of tears, furious with myself for not being able to catch and throw balls like other boys. For some reason it hit me how excluded and different I would always be because of my complete lack of skills.

"What's wrong with me?" I whined to my mother. "It can't be that hard. I'm not dumb. Why can't I figure it out?"

"What are you talking about?" she asked in complete bewilderment.

"Why can't I figure out how to play ball? Why does it seem so stupid to me, all these people acting like a ball is so important?"

"Important?" she repeated, completely baffled. "Of course, you don't understand," she scolded, "and that's why you can't play ball." She set down her iron on the end of the ironing board. "How could you? You refuse to join the other boys down at the playfield. You don't play with them, so of course you don't understand what they're talking about and you don't know how to play. You're always down in the basement with your nose in a book."

"I am not!" I said in ridiculous defiance, since it was so obviously true.

My mother wasn't listening. She was past that. She had unplugged the iron and was on her way to solving the problem. Opening the closet door, she took out a bat, a ball, and two gloves. "Come on." She swung open the back door, and left the screen door whooshing behind her.

"I don't want to," I whined. "Don't Mom, please."

But she was already outside, waiting for me.

"Get over there," she said in her no-nonsense Sicilian voice, planting her feet at one end of the patio, pointing toward the other end. Dreading what I could see was about to happen, I trailed after her and past her across the backyard, moving reluctantly toward where her finger was pointing.

She tossed one of the gloves across the patio toward me. I managed to catch it in a frantic fumble. "Put it on."

I did, gingerly, like I was scared it was infested with spiders.

"Now, look at me and listen."

I knew better than to argue. I looked at her, and listened.

"Keep your eye on the ball," she said. "Always. Don't get distracted. Focus on what I'm telling you. Keep your eye on the ball. Now, watch!" and threw it at me. I reached out the glove. The ball sailed past me, and crashed into the garden fence behind me.

"Concentrate," she said, as I retrieved the ball and tossed it back underhand to her. "Do you hear me? Watch the ball, and concentrate."

It sailed past me, rattling the fence with its impact.

"You're not concentrating."

"Yes, I am!"

It was an ordeal from hell. "Now, concentrate!" she'd order. Then she would throw the ball at me. I would reach bravely for it, fumble it, drop it. "You're not concentrating."

She was right, of course. I wasn't. How could anyone concentrate, looking at his mother's face slowly turning red with frustration? I'd throw it back over her head, or up the driveway, or straight into the garden.

"Look at me when you're throwing it. You're closing your eyes. Now, watch the ball and catch it."

I dropped it.

"You're not watching it."

She became exasperated. "Okay, let's try something different. Now focus." She pitched the ball easily to me. I swung the bat and missed. She threw it again. "Concentrate!" she shouted. "You're not concentrating!"

"I'm trying!" I shouted back, starting to cry with frustration.

"Stop crying and watch the ball," scolded my mother.

"I'm trying," I wailed.

"Okay, put the bat down," she conceded, after ten minutes of torture. "Let's concentrate on catching."

"But I can't."

"Yes, you can."

"Mom…"

"Yes, you can. Now, concentrate."

My father came home to find both his wife and his son with tears streaming down their faces in the back yard, desperately playing catch.

PART THREE

Chapter 14
Fifth Grade Honors

Most of life's big turning points we can see steaming in our direction from a long ways off, chugging and puffing toward us at a predictable pace, but every once in a while a life-altering development intrudes into our busy schedule that is not part of the game plan, smacking into us unannounced, knocking us off our habitual tracks and sending our lives careening in an unexpected direction.

Without any anticipation or forewarning, halfway through that summer of 1957 a letter arrived from Mark McGrath, principal of Maple Elementary School, addressed to my parents. It announced, to their surprise and delight, that because of my high scholastic achievements in my fourth grade year, I had been selected to be one of the twenty-four students included in a special honors program during the 1957-1958 academic year.

As an educational experiment, the highest scoring fifth graders were going to be combined with the highest scoring sixth graders into a special honors program, sharing the same classroom, learning separate subjects on opposite sides of the room but occasionally doing projects together.

"We're so proud he's been chosen to be in the program," said my mother, the next time the Simonetti sisters stopped by. Since we were in the middle of lunch, my brother and I were allowed to remain at the kitchen table as Dolores and Tamara came in through the back door and pulled up chairs for coffee.

"Did Sandra get a letter, too?" my mother asked ingenuously.

Tamara flushed. She had to set down her mug before it spilled. No letter had arrived yet regarding Sandra. She was still blushing and stammering, trying to regain her footing, when her sister, Dolores, interjected, "Yes, but I heard that program is going to be taught by a Jap."

I dropped my fork in shock. It clattered noisily on my plate. We didn't talk that way in our house. I was sputtering to hear such a racist comment, but my mother's fierce glare silenced any word of objection in my throat.

"I've heard she's a very good teacher," said Mom, looking at a far spot on the kitchen wall. Dolores and Tamara looked down at their coffee mugs, and quickly drained them. They left shortly after.

We knew perfectly well who would be teaching the course. The enterprising teacher who would orchestrate this brave new format in education was the beautiful and mysterious new teacher, Helen Yorozu.

She had arrived at Maple School the year before, the same as I did. I had seen Mrs Yorozu in the school halls and at an assembly where she presented an award. She was about as graceful and lovely as a teacher could be. We were in awe of her. Now I think back and realize this was just ten years after the war with Japan, and the forced imprisonment of Japanese-Americans on the west coast in internment camps. If she had lived here in Seattle, that would have meant her, too. Since I had grown up on Beacon Hill, I was used to going to school with kids of all races. I didn't notice her race. I noticed her beauty.

She would be assisted in teaching our honors class by Mr Trimm, the handsome sixth grade teacher, a soft-spoken, crewcut man in his thirties who would take our class out onto the playfield each day for physical education, and by Senor Nogales, the bright-eyed, warm-hearted Argentinean who would take over our classroom for an hour each day, during which the only language spoken would be Spanish. We would also have three hour-long periods each week upstairs in the Maple library, doing research on a project of our own devising under the inspired supervision of the school librarian, the hefty but surprisingly spry Mrs Hayes.

I would be included among some of the school's most popular students in a revolutionary education program taught by some of the school's most beloved teachers. I could hardly wait for summer to end, for the fall morning when I would walk the two blocks to school on the first day of class.

Only one person was unhappy by my placement in the honors program. My freckled neighbor, David Starr, who had introduced me to science fiction and had kept me company through two lonely summers, had not been invited into the honors program. We had gone through Fourth Grade together, eaten lunch together, hung around after school together, but we would no longer be in the same class.

"No big deal, we'll still see each other," he had laughed it off and shrugged. "Nothing's going to change." He was wrong. Everything changed. Our relaxed companionship with each other slowly stiffened, became brittle, and died. David Starr was my first lost friendship.

All that following year, when we happened to see each other out on the playfield at recess, we avoided looking each other in the eye. Neither one of us would cross the playfield to approach the other.

Chapter 15
The Faces of Portable Five

But if I was leaving behind one old friend, I was entering a brave new world teeming with social potential. The excitement among the honors students was tangible on both sides of the aisle that divided Portable Five. Many of the fifth graders I already knew from last year, a roll-call of the best and the brightest. But it was the older students who fascinated me. From just going to school there I already knew the names of a number of them.

Mary Steinberger was probably the single most popular girl at Maple Elementary, a pretty blonde with her hair pulled tight in a severe ponytail who got the highest grades in the school. Her clothes were always new and expensive, attractive but tasteful. She held the school record for walking the balance beam fifty-two times without falling. She was clean-cut and polite, one of those near-perfect people who probably suffer secretly from inner conflicts we can't even imagine.

Her thing was science. That got her excited. She was perpetually engrossed in one elaborate science experiment after another. I remember her project showing how a normal human tooth disintegrated in Coca-Cola. Her handsome display featured a row of test-tubes each containing two inches of Coke, as well as a tooth in the bottom of each of them at a different stage of decomposition, all carefully labeled and dated.

"Now, take a look at this tooth," she said dramatically in her first oral presentation, pointing an accusing finger at one of the test-tubes. "Take a good look, if you can stand it. Imagine that tooth is in your mouth. It's been in this bottle of Coke for one week. It's being eaten alive."

For years afterward I would refuse to drink Coke.

Most impressive of all was her hall display on the nature of germs, with petrie dishes overflowing with multiplying guck.

She was always kind to me. She was kind to everyone.

Craig Barker was also blond and popular, but there the similarity ended. He was determined to be a lawyer, and everything he announced in class already sounded like a legal summation, a reasoned argument to prove that his position was correct, clearly stated to avoid lawsuits. He never dressed casually, but always wore a dress jacket, a long-sleeved shirt with a buttoned collar, and a necktie or bowtie, as though he were just stopping off briefly at class before heading downtown to his bank.

He was one of the smartest kids at Maple School, with national test scores to prove it. He was also cunning, clever, and perpetually muttering a running commentary on the ineptness of the teaching staff and bumbling human behavior in general. I was afraid of Craig. I always kept my distance. He was fascinating but dangerous. He could act bright and wholesome and straightforward for days at a time, but he was an unsettling fellow who might turn his savage humor on you at any moment, and his friendly, all-American smile could quickly change into a lethal, competitive grin.

He was seldom seen anywhere without Benjamin Grimes, a sarcastic comedian who had nothing pleasant to say about anyone. Bennie was the one in class who perpetually asked sarcastic questions and made rude noises in the back of the room. Bennie was shorter, heavier, with pasty skin and a sour smile, but a savage wit that was instantaneous and lethal. The two of them were always snickering, as though something about you that you were unaware of was pathetically funny, like your zipper was down or you didn't realize you'd sat in something. Maybe because people were afraid of incurring their animosity, Craig and Bennie remained two of the school's most popular boys.

There was sophisticated, immaculate Lily Woo, never caught off-guard, never at a loss for words, and earthy, red-haired Carmen Johansen, with her mouthful of enormous teeth always on display in her gigantic smiles, and shy, attractive Brian Wilcox from Kansas.

However, the guy I was most excited to be in the same class with wasn't a sixth grader at all. He was a fellow fifth grader, a quiet new kid who had arrived at the end of last year in the spring, too late to really meet anyone, often standing alone at recess. I'd never dared to go up to him.

Though I was able to talk easily with almost anyone, around Jimmy Kersher I could think of nothing to say, inhibited by the sheer intensity of my attraction to him. Since he was in the other fourth grade room, our paths only crossed at recess, when there were several hundred shouting, screaming other complications to deal with in too short a time to engineer meeting someone new.

Whenever he came up in other kids' conversations, I would listen intently, and even ask a question or two without betraying too much interest. Slowly I had pieced together a picture. He was part of a poor family that had just moved into St. George's parish, because Bernadette had seen the Kersher family on the church's charity list. He came from somewhere in the South. Bernadette thought it might be Kentucky or Arkansas. He was part of a "broken home," with only a mother to care for three children.

It was a pure boyhood case of stunned moonstruck admiration, beyond sexual, because I hardly understood what sexual was. I don't remember how it started. I can't remember ever feeling anything less than awe in his presence.

He had as lean and flat a body as an eleven-year-old could possess, broad bony shoulders over a trim waist, skinny and awkward with his crew-cut over a big round head. He had a candid, open face and immaculately trimmed sideburns that were long enough to be noticed. Jimmy Kersher kept mostly to himself, soft-spoken, charmingly courteous and surprisingly smart. He never spoke to me. He acted like he didn't know who I was. No matter how often I saw him on the playground, he never smiled or said hello, seemed utterly oblivious to my presence.

As for me, I couldn't keep my eyes off him.

I was obsessed with him, the way he looked, the way he stood or sat or leaned in doorways. He was a lovely marvel of coordination and proportion and sheer youthful physical exuberance, with much to admire and fascinating to watch. But I didn't really fall in love with Jimmy Kersher until I saw him run.

Watching him dash across the playfield was a revelation. It was a joy to behold, pure physical poetry to see how his body moved, so graceful and economical, so limber and aerodynamic. He was faster than any other pupil at Maple, held the record in both the sprint and the quartermile.

And he ran in a distinctive way. His legs look huge leaps forward with gazelle-like grace, but what you remembered most were those big, bony hands, hanging loosely at the wrist, like flags or banners, as he hurtled forward. Where most boys ran clenching their fingers into fists, Jimmy Kersher left his hands loose and flapping.

Whenever he ran across the playfield, I would forget what I was doing and turn to watch.

Chapter 16
Teahouse of the August Moon

Seen in retrospect, looking back on that year from today, the woman responsible for my great awakening remains an enigma. Mrs Yorozu never mentioned internment camps, and in fact, at the time I had no idea there had ever been such horrible things. No bitterness could be glimpsed in her, and yet she must have been confined to the camps as a child. Surely her parents had been mistreated. She must have known people who had suffered in them. How could she be without a flicker of resentment?

Instead I only remember her as one of the most dedicated teachers I ever had, an instructor who made me feel I was personally important to her. Soon I found myself spellbound by the kind firmness with which she conducted herself. Quietly, gracefully, Helen Yorozu kept her class in rapt attention.

And that was before she made her shocking, awe-inspiring announcement.

"Class, let me ask you something," she began, on the day she caught us all by surprise. "Give me a show of hands. How many of you have ever been to a live theater production?"

My hand went up into the air, but I was one of very few. I had been to see several live plays because Nana had taken us downtown on the bus to the old Palomar Theater, to attend productions of the Seattle Junior Programs on Saturday morning. They were only amateur productions catering to children, and all but one are lost to memory. Of that one show, however, *The Wizard of Oz*, one moment remains alive in my memory. Dorothy and her companions violated all my childhood expectations midway through the performance by coming down off the stage and right out into the audience, trying to find their way out of the poppy field.

"Goodness," said Mrs Yorozu, "well then, let me tell you that theater is a magic art because it happens right in front of you. It's better than a movie, because it's alive, and it's slightly different every night it's performed. Some people love theater, and go to many plays. You'll be surprised, some of you in this classroom may grow up to be the very kind of people who buy season tickets to a theatre in town."

How far-fetched that seemed then, how true her words became.

"Well, what many people don't know is most actors don't make very much money. Movie stars do, but most regular actors have to work day jobs as well as acting jobs. Actors are just ordinary people like your parents except that they have two jobs instead of one, a job for money and a job for love."

We had no idea where any of this was leading, until she revealed her secret. "Well, I am one of those people with two jobs. And what I do when I am not here teaching you is perform in plays. I'm an actress."

Mrs Yorozu was so utterly poised and confident that this news should have surprised no one. The surprise came next. "Why am I telling you this now? Because every night for the last two weeks, when I've left this school at the end of the day, instead of going home, I've gone to rehearsal at a theater here in town, where I rehearse until ten o'clock at night. I hardly see my poor husband. And why? Because I've landed a wonderful role in a play that opens this next Thursday night. The name of the play is *Teahouse of the August Moon*. It's a famous comedy about soldiers in the war, and the name of the theater performing it is the Cirque. The amazing thing about the Cirque is that it's different from ordinary theaters – the stage is in the middle, and the audience sits all around it."

This was so much information about a world I knew nothing about that my head was spinning.

"And now, here's the best part. Next Wednesday night there is going to be a dress rehearsal of the play. The very first complete performance, with the set and the costumes and the music all together for the first time. And because you are my students, you are all invited to come that night for free. Whoever would like to attend, and can bring a note from their parents, can enjoy watching their teacher be an actress in a very good play."

Could there be anything so exciting? I was thunderstruck to think this marvelous teacher also had an alternate life on stage. I rushed home, and my parents were happy to write the required note.

Our whole class went. To our stunned amazement, our teacher performed the leading female role of Lotus Blossom. She wore beautiful kimonos and performed all kinds of exotic rituals.

I wore my best Sunday dress suit and sat in the second row of the round auditorium. I went into a trance. The actors were so close! All my defenses were blown away. We all stood up cheering at the end when Mrs Yorozu took her bow. For the rest of my life I would never recover from my infatuation with theater.

Chapter 17
Touchdowns and Fly Balls

Every day I walked to school in suspense, not knowing what would lie ahead. Learning with older kids in the room was extremely provocative. I found myself constantly showing off and competitive, trying to be the first one to raise his hand with the answer to Mrs Yorozu's questions, trying to get the highest scores on the tests. My spelling, grammar, and language skills ranked neck-and-neck right up there with Mary Steinberger at the top of the class.

My downfall was physical education, one of the few subjects not taught by Mrs Yorozu, but presided over by the manly, soft-spoken Mr Trimm. Unlike many men with coaching skills, Mr Trimm wasn't a bully and didn't frighten me. Having failed so miserably in Little League, I tried extra hard to please him. Strangely enough, he seemed to respond to my obvious sincerity with a patience that was considerate, respectful, and very well-intended. That it had no apparent result was unjust. I should have improved. I should have blossomed. Other boys did.

I remember the one sport I wasn't too awful at was dodgeball, played in the big cement-enclosed room we called our gym, a cavernous vault gouged into the side of the school which was exactly like the building's loading dock without the dock, just three walls of cement and a cyclone fence all along one wall, exposing us to the elements with some shelter from the rain. The gym had a terrible echo, and the loud smacking of the rubber ball on all three walls made head-ringing, deafening noise, along with the unavoidable screaming and shouting of frenzied participants.

I wasn't too bad at dodgeball. At least not until I was hit in the head. I never found out who aimed it at me. It was clearly on purpose. Though it was only a big rubber ball, the rubber was hard, it hit me square in the nose, and it smacked into me at high velocity, knocking me off my feet. Though I scampered back up and shook off everyone's laughter, it hurt my pride, my nose, and my butt, and left me slightly gun-shy toward balls in general.

I have two memories of Mr Trimm, both involving balls.

The first occurred at a football game we played on the upper playfield, fifth graders against sixth graders. Patiently helping me figure out what to do, Mr Trimm made me a guard, showed me how to stand on the line all hunched over and ferocious, taught me how to plow ahead into the opposing guard on the other team, and not to worry about hurting them.

I remember that afternoon the sky had begun to grow dark, the score was tied, it looked like it was going to downpour any second. I'd guarded well, although early in the game I'd fumbled an easy catch. Team spirits were high and I was part of those spirits. The first drops of rain had just started to fall when the ball came flying toward me over my shoulder. I saw Craig Barker jumping up to catch the pass.

Before I knew what I was doing, I'd leaped up and intercepted the ball.

Screams of outrage. I took off in terror, clutching the ball to my chest, as the sky darkened and rain came down in sheets. Shoulders came hurtling toward me. I dodged, I scrambled, I nearly slipped, I flung myself past them all, ignored the shouts, forced my lungs to take big gulps of air, until I charged across the line and through the goalposts.

I turned around expecting the glory of victory, only to be met by shrieks of hilarity and furious contempt. I had run the wrong way. I had won the game for the sixth graders.

I returned utterly humiliated and drenched to the classroom with Craig and Bennie's mocking laughter pursuing me like a curse.

The second memory is of Mr. Trimm at home plate during fielding practice, hitting balls to us on the diamond and in the outfield. Right field was where I could cause the least harm, which was where I was usually placed, and where rival teams would always do their best to direct their hits, once they saw me standing out there in terror.

That day Mr Trimm was hitting balls to each of us, giving us all practice, one by one. Usually he wore a necktie and dress jacket, but for outdoor events he took off his jacket and unbuttoned his collar and rolled up his sleeves. He'd throw the ball carelessly up in the air, then bring around the bat gracefully one-handed and bop one to the first baseman, now to the shortstop, now to left field, and then it was my turn.

It was a high fly ball.

I rushed to the center of right field, so I was standing directly beneath it, stood there cowering behind my baseball glove, held up to protect me, waiting for gravity to reclaim the ball, desperately hoping it would land in the pocket of my outthrust glove.

No such luck. The ball hit me in the forehead.

I don't remember that. The next thing I remember is feeling like I was falling into the sky, then realizing I was lying on my back on the playfield staring up at the clouds with a terrible headache, with Mr Trimm bending over me looking very concerned. He helped me to my feet, held me in his strong arms, against his warm chest where I could hear his pounding heart. He examined my forehead.

"Does it hurt?"

I wanted to say yes. I wanted to say no. I didn't say anything.

He looked me in the eye. Then he probed my forehead gently with his fingertips, as though feeling for a crack.

"Better have the nurse look at that," he said, without any incriminating comment or smart-alecky disclaimer, no scolding or mockery. Instead, he said, "Can you walk?" and when I didn't reply at first... Did he really carry me into the school in his arms, my cheek against the buttons of his shirt, or is that simply what I was hoping would happen?

I do remember lying in the nurse's tiny office, tucked around the corner behind the front desk, stretched out underneath a glass-fronted cabinet containing an ax for use in case of fire, and looking up at Mr Trimm standing beside the narrow single bed. I remember the ax being there, because I thought, "I could accidentally hit my head on that cabinet, and make the ax fall out on top of me and kill myself."

Mr Trimm distracted me from my fears. He took my hand, and gave it a hearty squeeze. "No damage done," he said cheerfully. "Thinking faculties unimpaired?"

He looked at me like he expected an answer. When I failed to generate one, he winked, gave me an analytical look, and straightened his glasses on his nose. "You seem to have quite the head for sports, young man," he said, smiling broadly, pleased with himself at his own droll sense of humor. "Something about your head seems to attract flying objects, particularly balls."

Chapter 18
Hiroshima

Book reports were my favorite part of classroom activity. Since reading had become such an obsession of mine, writing about books was effortless. Reading is such a solitary pleasure! When it works, a good book compels the reader to break out of that solitude and become social, to urge the experience on others. I always wanted to tell everyone when I discovered a good new book, like *Sword at Sunset* or *Call It Courage* or *Caddie Woodlawn*.

Mrs Yorozu caught on to this immediately, and allowed me to have sporadic little five-minute classroom presentations, space fillers really, when she needed a few moments to prepare for the next subject of our instruction, and could do so while I rattled on to the class about the latest wonderful book I had discovered.

You like to hope you weren't too annoying. I might have been pretty full of myself. But I genuinely loved books and reading, and having a chance to speak my mind about them, trying to persuade others to take a chance on them, was a natural vocation. Especially the classics! For me, that meant the two fathers of science fiction, H. G. Wells and Jules Verne. I adored anything with Captain Nemo in it, especially *Mysterious Island*.

My favorite discovery that year was a thin paperback I actually purchased with my own money, written by a science fiction author I liked called Ray Bradbury, a book that wasn't science fiction called *Dandelion Wine*. It's the story of a young boy in a small town over the course of a summer. Until then I had always thought of summer as a frightening time, stranded among strangers without any friends to alleviate the hot loneliness. Then I read that book. I'd never read anything like it. It was like a spell that had captured a boy's summer. It was about simple joys that I had never even considered particularly happy events, like mowing the lawn or getting new sneakers.

I can get pretty worked up over a book. I became euphoric. The class clapped after I finished my presentation.

But the book report I remember most was the last, the one that went so sadly wrong. Usually I eagerly informed Mrs Yorozu when I had a book report to give. That time I hadn't told her yet, and I don't remember exactly why, but I wasn't expecting to talk. She addressed me directly in class, and caught me by surprise.

"Now, I may be wrong, but I suspect I know someone who has a new book he'd like to tell us about…"

I had just finished reading a superb book, so I couldn't resist going up there to just extemporize and hope for the best. I could speak about books easily enough. I stood beside her desk in the front of the class, turned around to face everyone, and started out as I always did, confident and filled with my usual urgent enthusiasm.

"The book I've just finished reading is by John Hersey and it's called *Hiroshima*. It came out eleven years ago in 1946, one year after we dropped the atom bomb on Japan. The *New Yorker* dedicated one full issue to it, with no cartoons. Then it was printed as a book by the Book of the Month Club and given away for free because it was so important."

I had the class's complete attention.

"It was the scariest thing I've ever read in my life. It freaked me out, it's so horrible. It's about six people who were actually there when we dropped the atom bomb on Hiroshima, what they saw and what they…"

That's all the farther I got.

Suddenly the whole idea of the bombing of Hiroshima was more than I could bear. It was like a delayed emotional response to a whole city full of people being burned alive, a concept that had short-circuited my child-size imagination. I got too choked up to continue. A soggy wet sound came out of my throat. My eyes filled with tears, and I stood there stupefied and embarrassed and gasping for air, for one of the few times in my life without a word to say, my mouth opening and shutting but nothing coming out.

In panic I happened to look at Mrs Yorozu, and the look in her eyes is the one memory that will always haunt me. It was pain, yes, it was certainly pain, but it was pain in an entirely different dimension than what I was feeling, pain that came from knowledge. Pain for what? Pain for the victims of the nuclear blast? Was it something personal? Some loved one lost in the bombing?

Sheer pain registered in her eyes, and nothing more.

"You can sit down," she said to me graciously, allowing me time to clumsily regain my chair. "The atom bomb is a terrible, terrible thing, and if you think about it for a moment too long, it can leave anyone speechless. Let's open our math books now to page 159..."

Chapter 19
Behind the Baseball Backstop

Whenever I gave my book talks, the boy who clapped the loudest and the longest was Fritz Wachter. Though we were the same age, he'd been in the other fourth grade class the year before. Other than hearing his name, which was unusual, our paths had never crossed.

He surprised quite a few people by managing to get into the experimental honors program. Fritz wasn't exactly what you'd call honors material. Curiosity over his surprising inclusion was ultimately satisfied by Stephanie Powers, whose older sister worked as a filing assistant in the office and had access to all the teachers' grade books. According to her, Fritz Wachter had just barely squeaked by, the lowest grade point on the fifth grade rostrum to be included in the bunch.

"Then how did he get in?" everyone wanted to know, and Stephanie's answer was always the same.

"Mrs Bates," she would say, with a shrug of her shoulders, as though just saying the name of the school counselor were enough to explain the silliness of the entire situation. Mary Elizabeth Bates was a good-hearted bubblehead whose unfounded cheer and optimism were legendary among students and faculty alike. "She thinks that Fritz has *promise*."

Mrs Bates would certainly be in a position to know, since Fritz had spent more than his share of time in the counselor's office. But the promise simply never happened. After that year in the honors program Fritz would fall from grace and popularity and virtually disappear from any surviving memories. But that year, in Portable Five, he was an irrepressible, mischievous rascal who often brought a high-flying conversation down to earth with a thud of delightful common sense, and frequently caused the entire class to erupt into laughter, even Mrs Yorozu doing her best to keep a straight face.

His attention was sought by everyone. His company guaranteed hours of laughter. He had a puckish impulse to provoke reactions, a rascal's sense of humor, combined with a bit of an elfish look, with unruly, straw-colored hair and a grin that always looked like he'd just heard a good off-color joke. His voice had a gravelly earthiness, a sandy, crackling sound that made even the simplest statement sound wiser than it was. His pale blue eyes were tiny and far apart, and always looked like they'd been either laughing or crying, slightly swollen around the lids, hiding something in their depths.

Inexplicably Fritz chose to bestow his friendship upon me. He'd catch my glance toward the back of the classroom, and give me a comic wink. He'd wait till I was watching him, and then silently mime falling asleep while Mrs Yorozu was speaking, collapsing into silent snores on his desk. He'd chum along with me at recess. He'd ask my opinion on any number of topics. He'd sit down beside me on the grassy banks surrounding the playground during lunch break, and offer me half of whatever candy bar his mother had dropped in his lunch bag. He'd report on his favorite TV shows from the night before. He'd save his best new jokes to tell me first.

The explanation for these honors was not long in coming. Like most boys in our school, Fritz had a crush on Sandra Bergamini. The difference was that Fritz had decided to do something about it. If he could just draw her into the circle of his charms, he was sure he could make a lasting impression. Fritz had an effervescent self-confidence that was highly persuasive. He was so delighted with himself that the attitude was catching. As far as he was concerned, enchanting her would be the easy part. All he needed was an opportunity to expose her to his charms. And to facilitate that end, he pursued my friendship. He had seen Sandra and me clowning around together.

I was his ticket to Sandra.

He was aware that my house was near Sandra's, and that our families knew each other. He could see that Sandra trusted me. Realizing I could be a key player, he had watched me carefully, and it couldn't have been too hard to figure me out. Fritz had a natural talent for noticing opportunities that furthered his cause and a bold ruthlessness that enabled him to take advantage of them.

It must have been easy to spot my secret adoration. As soon as I was within five feet of Jimmy Kersher, I became tongue-tied. I could approach anyone else easily, but became sweaty and nervous at the very mention of his name.

Without my noticing or even suspecting, he had been smart enough to see through my performance and realize that Jimmy Kersher mattered to me insanely much, that I would do just about anything to possess his friendship, but was too shy to pursue him on my own.

That would be Fritz's ace. He had what I wanted. Jimmy Kersher was his friend.

Fritz and Jimmy had grown up together in a bad neighborhood. They'd toughed it out in a rough crowd of kids, most of whom would soon be selling drugs, robbing convenience stores, in prison, or dead. Fritz and Jimmy had escaped from the old neighborhood and stood a chance of being among its survivors.

He began talking about Jimmy Kersher more often. I would see them at recess together. Obviously Fritz had Jimmy's trust. Out on the playground Fritz was one of the only people I'd ever seen Jimmy talk to. Maybe Fritz secretly admired him, too. Who wouldn't? Maybe we were both smitten. Regardless, because of Fritz's close alliance with Jimmy, I accepted his advances.

As for Jimmy, he seemed to be completely oblivious to me. If Fritz ever mentioned me, Jimmy gave no sign of it. I suspect he had no idea who I even was, much less that there was anyone at Maple School who was dying to become his friend.

One afternoon after school, just as it was starting to get dark, when you knew in your gut that it couldn't be far from dinnertime, as Fritz and I were walking back to where we had chained our bikes behind the backstop, he startled me by saying, "You really like Jimmy Kersher, don't you?"

I was so taken aback by his question that I didn't answer at first. I just kept on walking around behind the weathered gray boards of the baseball backstop, then hunched over my bike and focused on spinning the numbers on my combination lock, concentrating on unlocking my bike. An evening breeze had started to chill the afternoon. If I weren't just two blocks away from a warm home and dinner, I would have been cold. The only other kids on the playground were at the other end. Occasionally you could hear their shouts, but it was too far away to make out what they were saying.

"Don't you?" persisted Fritz. "I've been watching you. Jimmy Kersher, you really like him?"

Behind the backstop, unchaining our bikes, the two of us were completely out of sight. A gritty layer of dirt underfoot had slid down from the sneaker-trampled banks that lined the cyclone fence behind us. The ground was littered with cigarette butts, a couple hardened wads of chewing gum, and a crushed red candy bar wrapper.

"I like him fine," I said finally. That was the best I could do.

He laughed. I wouldn't even look at him. "You like him a little more than fine," he said with disturbing confidence. He gave me time to say something. I didn't. "Am I not supposed to notice?"

I tried to think of how I might have betrayed my secret obsession. "When did you notice that?"

Fritz grinned. "Every time Jimmy comes anywhere near you. He's a pretty guy, I admit it. His belly muscles are incredible."

That got my attention. No one had ever spoken to me about my obsession before. I couldn't resist participating. "I've never seen his belly muscles," I had to admit, choking out the words, trying to suppress the sheer wanting that dripped from every syllable.

Fritz cackled with confidence. "Oh, wait till you do. His belly muscles are the best." He acted like he could see them right now in front of him, hesitating just a moment to admire them, long enough for me to imagine just how sweet that must feel to actually touch them, and then to calculate how long I would have to wait before that glorious opportunity might possibly present itself. "You know, he would let you feel them."

I could hardly believe I was hearing right. "You think he'd let me feel his belly muscles?"

"If I asked him to let you, he would."

Now the serpent lays the conditions. How shameful and desperate, that it would come to that. Inevitably, sooner or later, Fritz and I were doomed to realize that all we had to do was trade favors: he'd be happy to set up an arrangement with Jimmy Kersher, and in exchange I would be expected to help him realize his dream of charming Sandra.

His offer called into question just how much my friendship with Sandra was worth. Was I above betraying her, selling her trust in exchange for an opportunity to feel the exquisite skin and supple body underneath Jimmy Kersher's shirt?

"Why would you ask him to let me do that?"

"Because you're my friend," said Fritz, his face lighting up with a grin. "Friends help each other, don't they?"

Chapter 20
The Kissing Game

Put two memories side by side, and they can seem to suggest cause and effect. They may have nothing to do with each other. They just tend to lump together logically, whether they happened that way or not.

I don't remember whether the kissing game was a direct result of my bargain with Fritz, but inventing a game was nothing unusual for me. I was constantly inventing games, unfortunately games which showed only too clearly my own pent-up desires, and this was the first of several games for which I would get in trouble. I invented a game at the beach where I was the roaring Creature from the Black Lagoon who got to attack the bare-skinned participating cousins and drag them underwater, squirming and wrestling. I invented a game where we boy cousins locked ourselves into one of the bedrooms, unbuttoned our shirts, and took turns shooting and dying on each other. In light of these more obvious self-gratifying sports, the kissing game showed some restraint and didn't actually satisfy my own needs.

But then maybe I invented it for Fritz.

At recess time we would check out a jump-rope. Instead of the more traditional way of jumping rope, with one person at either end swinging it in circles while a third in the center jumps, we used the rope circle-style, with only one person at the center in charge of swinging it. Always preferring to be facilitator rather than participant, that person was me. I would stand in the middle and swing the jump rope in a swishing mandala, around and around about six inches off the ground, while those playing the game were gathered about me, jumping to avoid the rope.

I can't remember the rules or logic of the game. Perhaps it didn't have any. The penalty for those who were hit by the rope was that they could be immediately kissed by any other jumper. I can't quite remember the point here, how only one person got kissed per game when you would think everyone who got hit by the rope would get kissed – or even, how kissing could possibly be considered a penalty for anything or what prevented some people from being kissed by more than one person.

How frustrating when memory simply fails you! I have no explanation. The game seems to depend on a child's sense of kissing as being icky, but there's an uncomfortable edge of testosterone to the sexual aggression of the victory. It started with just Fritz and me and a couple girls. Soon others were joining us. Fritz was the uncontested champion. He clowned around as he jumped, and made it look like a really fun time. And, of course, Fritz was always very enthusiastic about the kissing part.

The game became more and more popular. It was daring and sexy, and it rapidly became notorious. Kids at recess had to start waiting in line to play because the circle of jumpers became too crowded.

How could this game have been designed to fulfill my part of the bargain with Fritz? It seems far-fetched. Yet that's how I remember it. Surely we couldn't force Sandra Bergamini to play the game with us. Could we possibly have been so cunning that we invented a game to lure her and trap her?

We were eleven. That kind of plotting is hard to believe.

So maybe it was just sheer luck that brought Sandra Bergamini and two other pretty girls from Georgetown to the kissing game. Maybe it was sheer luck that Fritz and I were the game's initiators. Sandra asked us a few coy questions, and then stood off with her friends making up her mind, while Fritz and I gave each other the eye. After several laughing hesitations and delays, Sandra and her friends decided to watch a round of the game first. So they stepped back and I started spinning the rope around in a circle. The game was simple and quick, with a couple near misses, and ended in a comical kiss between two friends and much laughter.

The game looked fun and harmless.

With a little tittering between themselves, Sandra and one of the other girls stepped forward to play. Fritz and I didn't need to exchange any more signals. We waited in suspense as other jumpers stepped forward. We knew exactly what we were doing.

"Okay, everybody ready?"

Before Sandra can change her mind, we'd better start playing. Whether we planned it or not, this is the opportunity we've been waiting for. Now all I have to do is swing the rope exactly right.

"Here we go."

Around goes the rope, around and around until it gets up a good speed and hovers levelly above the asphalt.

"In!" I shout.

Everybody who's playing in this round of the game jumps closer, into range of the rope, and starts to negotiate it as it whistles around in a circle. When you're hit, you step out. Around goes the rope, striking ankles.

Out goes one.

Out goes another.

Fewer and fewer are jumping now, but these last half dozen are better jumpers, and now the rope begins to slowly speed up. Around goes the rope, a little faster.

And again, a little faster yet.

And then faster, and then faster.

Only two are left jumping, Sandra and Fritz.

And then faster than Sandra expected.

The moment the rope hit her ankles, Fritz broke away from his place in the circle and charged toward her. Sandra was still recovering from the shock of being hit by the rope, but the sight of Fritz leaping aggressively in her direction caused Sandra to bolt, with an angry squeal of exasperation. She was fast, but so was he. She was caught off-guard. He had been waiting to pounce. They ran across the upper playfield, down the stairs, and zigzagged around through the portables on the lower playfield until they were out of sight.

The kissing game screeched to a halt. We waited for them to return. Neither one did. We were just beginning to start another game when the bell rang.

Recess was over.

The rest of the day, I kept looking at Fritz's empty desk and chair and wondering what could have happened.

Chapter 21
Consequences

That night when the phone rang I was stretched out on the carpet reading in the living room while the rest of the family was watching television. My father and mother were enjoying their favorite sit-com, laughing out loud right along with the fake television audience, and my little brother was laughing along with them, whether he understood the jokes or not. Everyone was having such a good time no one seemed to notice I was reading.

The house telephone was anchored at the end of the drainboard in the kitchen. I had been hoping all night to get a call from Fritz. The phone had been silent. I could have phoned him, or I could have phoned Sandra. I had done neither. Maybe it wasn't my way to phone people. Maybe I was wary of showing too much interest in what happened between them. I don't have answers. You would think, now that it was finally ringing, I would have jumped up to answer it, but I was in darkest Africa in the middle of *King Solomon's Mines*, with no telephones anywhere near.

My mother's armchair was the closest, and as usual she was the one who pushed to her feet and trotted into the kitchen, voluntarily missing part of her favorite show. I was only peripherally aware of my mother getting up to answer the phone, until I heard her say, "Hi, Tamara," and realized the caller was Mrs Bergamini down the block.

Mother's voice dropped softer, so that I could no longer make out what she was saying. Although I continued to hold *King Solomon's Mines* as though I were still in the grips of the story, I had stopped reading. Over the top of the book cover I was watching her face. She asked a few questions. She listened. She stopped smiling and her features became grave. It wasn't hard to guess what she was being told. Tamara's daughter had been kissed by my friend, Fritz, in some nasty game I had invented where I spun the rope around in a circle and unfairly hit Sandra on the ankles.

My mother hung up, gave my father a nod. He looked forward every week to *The Dick Van Dyke Show*, and very reluctantly gave a last glance at the television before he joined her for a quiet conversation by the telephone. I was quietly panicking. I tried to read my book. I tried to enjoy Dick Van Dyke's rubber-boned physical comedy. Something happened on television and the fake audience roared, as though they'd never seen anything quite so funny in their lives.

My father stepped back into the living room and asked me to come join them. I'd had enough time to brace myself, but I was still trembling. My brother was left watching television alone as my father escorted me into the kitchen and pulled the sliding door shut.

My mother did not look happy. "Did you know that Sandra left school early today?"

"She did?"

I genuinely didn't know. All I knew was that Fritz had never returned to Portable Five. Hearing that Sandra had not returned, either, made me feel uncomfortably involved.

"Tamara says she came home crying."

Knowing Sandra, knowing how much her pride would have inhibited her from such an emotional display, chilled me with guilt.

"So you didn't know about her running home because some friend of yours ran after her, kissing her?"

"She ran home?" I repeated lamely. My eyes must have told my mother that I'd had no idea.

"Tamara said you were playing a game."

I nodded.

My father had stood by, letting my mother lead the inquiry, but chose now to cut to the essential issues. "Tell us about this game, and what exactly happened to Sandra."

I felt like a witness called to testify in a trial. "It's just a jump-roping game. It's no big deal. Why, what did she tell you?"

My mother ignored my question, and fired one of her own. "Did you have something to do with your friend kissing Sandra?"

"Of course not!"

My parents continued to look at me, waiting for me to tell the truth. That wasn't going to happen. Although sickened at having to lie to my parents, there was too much at stake for regrets. "What did she tell you, Mom? Did she say it was my fault that Fritz kissed her? That's crazy. How could it be my fault? I didn't even know it happened until just now."

My father sighed. "This jump-roping game with the kissing in it – was that your idea?"

As usual, he could cut through all the fluster and emotion and get to the one basic irrefutable point. "Yes," I admitted.

He shook his head sadly in disbelief. His voice was scarcely a whisper. "What possesses you?"

Having said that, having expressed his disappointment and incredulity at my poor behavior, he rose from his chair at the kitchen table and went back into the living room, welcomed by a burst of canned laughter, joining my brother in front of the television. It was a good question. I had jeopardized my friendship with Sandra, angered her parents, as well as angered my own – for what purpose, to what end? What possessed me?

Jimmy Kersher possessed me.

Chapter 22
Appointment at Midnight

Tamara's phone call that night was the first I heard that Fritz had enjoyed his part of the bargain. The next morning in school he winked at me across the classroom and gave me thumbs up. Then at the first recess, as soon as we were up on the playfield, he poured out all the details, much more than I was comfortable hearing, cackling with delight.

Sandra had not been amused to find that the kissing game had degenerated into a chase. She'd run in earnest. She was repelled by his advances. She'd scolded him, shouted at him, tried to push him away, but he'd kissed her, anyway. He got what he wanted, but had over-estimated his charms.

"Get away from me!"

"You think you're so pretty."

"You're so stupid, leave me alone."

"Don't be so mean. Give me a chance. Most girls like me."

"That's not what I've heard."

He had given her his famous mischievous grin, which usually won over anyone who was reluctant. It didn't work with Sandra. She failed to find him irresistible. She had shoved him in the chest, swore at him in Italian, made a face, and pretended to wipe off her lips on her sleeve, but what did that matter? He still came away the victor, didn't he?

He had stolen a kiss from Sandra Bergamini.

Though she wasn't in our class, I used to frequently see Sandra at recess. That recess I didn't see her anywhere, nor her two best friends. Not until after the bell rang and Fritz and I were walking back toward Portable Five did I glimpse her farther down the playfield just going up the steps to Portable Three.

"Sandra!"

She turned in my direction, and then turned sourly away without a word, her lips in a sullen pout. I felt guilty for even being seen with Fritz. She knew I had betrayed her, she just didn't know why. I tried to ignore the ugly feeling that knowledge left inside me.

But I wasn't so filled with guilty repentance that I was willing to ignore the conditions of our bargain. My half of the agreement had now been fulfilled. It was time for me to get my half of the rewards.

Fritz didn't make me wait. As though he could read my mind, he came over to me the minute the final bell rang, as Mrs Yorozu sank down into her chair and began gathering together the papers on her desk and all our classmates went shoving and crowding out the portable door into the freedom of the afternoon.

Bumping shoulders as we headed out the door together, in that raspy voice of his that always sounded like he was on the edge of snickering, he told me that he was on his way over to Jimmy Kersher's house to talk to him about our deal.

I nodded in acknowledgement and grunted and tried to act nonchalant, while my heart went soaring. I couldn't bring myself to go home. I loitered around the playground for over an hour, hoping Fritz would pass that way again and set my heart at peace, pretending to be interested in after-school games while I waited, counting the number of baskets dunked at the nearby hoop.

Fritz never came back through the schoolyard.

That night after dinner I was downstairs reading *Journey to the Center of the Earth* for the third time by a single dim light in my bedroom when there was a sharp rattling knock at the basement window. It startled me so badly I dropped the paperback and lost my place. Someone had stepped down into the window-well and was knocking on the glass with his shoe.

I jumped up onto my bed and wrenched open the curtain to find myself looking up at Fritz.

"Open up, it's cold out here."

I ran around to the laundry room and let him in quietly through the basement door. Stepping through the sheets hung up to dry on the clotheslines that crisscrossed the laundry room ceiling, he came quietly back to my bedroom with me and waited till I'd closed the door.

"He'll meet you at the backstop at midnight."

"Midnight?" I repeated. "I can't meet him at midnight. What am I supposed to tell my folks?"

He looked at me like I'd just delivered a laugh-line, and not delivered it well. He shook his head, clearly considered my case hopeless, and looked like he was ready to turn around and leave. His windbreaker was zipped up to his chin, the jacket collar was up around his neck, and he reeked of beer and pizza.

"Tell your folks? Do you have to tell them anything?" said Fritz. "I thought you said you lived by yourself down here."

"I do, but…"

"Well, didn't I just come through the basement door?"

"Of course you did, but…"

"Did your parents notice?"

"I don't think so, but…"

"Are you going to tell your parents I was here?"

"Of course not, but…"

"Do your parents come down and check your bed during the night to make sure you're in it?"

"No, no, no, they would never do anything like that."

Fritz grinned at my thick-headedness. "And you do know how to close a door quietly, so that it doesn't wake anyone up?"

I nodded, out of objections.

"So then, I don't understand. What's to stop you from being at the backstop at midnight?"

With a cackle at my mental slowness, he was already heading back down the hall toward the laundry room, through the damp white maze of sheets, reaching for the knob of the basement door. He turned around in the open doorway to blind me with his mischievous rascal smile. "Unless you're trying to say that you don't want to feel his belly muscles?"

"No, no, I do, I do, but…"

"I thought so." He didn't even say good-night, he just closed the door soundlessly behind him and scampered off into the darkness. I stood watching him go, my heart pounding at the thought that there was no turning back, that the deal was in place, dying with curiosity wondering what in the world Jimmy Kersher must think of me now, ashamed of wanting to touch him so badly, unable to resist doing it.

Chapter 23
The Betrayal

At nine o'clock I said good-night to Mom, Dad and my brother as usual and then went downstairs to my bedroom. There I lay on the bed, wide-eyed and sleepless, waiting for my midnight appointment. The minutes dragged. Time stopped. My heart beat insanely loudly, and I thought I might die. I tried to go back to reading my Jules Verne paperback but I couldn't concentrate, listening to every footfall and creak of the floorboards upstairs, waiting impatiently until everyone else had finally turned off the television and gone to bed. Briefly I heard my parents' murmuring voices in the bedroom above me. Then the last toilet flush gurgled through the pipes, and the house became silent. I checked my watch. Shortly after eleven.

I waited until a quarter to midnight.

Then I pulled on my jeans and a sweatshirt in the dark and quietly slipped out the basement door without anyone hearing me. It was a huge act of sneaky disobedience for a boy who invariably played by the rules like I did. It was like nothing I had ever dared to do before. Until now I had maintained confidence in myself by doing the socially correct thing. Now I was throwing righteous conduct out the window in a risky act of self-indulgence.

The night-darkened familiar world of our neighborhood street loomed as unpredictable and treacherous, the shadows no longer benign and encouraging like good neighbors, the sidewalks endangered by untended bushes with spidery overhanging branches scratching for my eyes, by sidewalk cracks and inequities of root-broken cement slabs reaching out to trip me. I could hear my footfalls slapping down the deserted sidewalk. The rustle of my sweatshirt, my heavy breathing, everything seemed to make too much noise in the still, still night. I'd never been to Maple School that late before. The playground was hushed and deserted. I'd timed it perfectly, arriving at the backstop a few minutes early. It was precisely seven minutes to midnight.

It was too dark and way too quiet. The lure of meeting with Jimmy Kersher had been irresistible, but I had never before defied the sensible rules of my parents and our household. My heart was pounding in panic. Was this kind of defiance the first step in the long road to evil? Was I taking an irrevocable step that I would regret for the rest of my life? I was scared of the dark, scared of what I couldn't see, but I wanted to feel his belly muscles enough to bravely wait for him there, nervously peering into the darkness in every direction as I paced back and forth, again and again squinting at the hands of my watch to see if it was midnight yet, shivering in the chilly night breeze.

Then across the darkened playground I saw someone walking toward me, toward where I was waiting by the baseball backstop. He walked up to me, and for a moment neither of us knew what to say.

"Hi."

"Hi."

I was mentally dogpaddling. I had no idea what was appropriate, had no idea what exactly Fritz had told him, couldn't come up with a single thing to say. Several moments passed while neither of us said another word or made the slightest move.

Jimmy Kersher was dressed the way he always was, faded low-slung jeans and a T-shirt that had once been white, no jacket, no accommodation to the chill of the night. The light of the streetlamp on the corner sharpened the line of his sideburn against his cheek. We just listened to one another breathing and stood watching each other, waiting. Then Jimmy talked first, and what he said caught me completely by surprise.

"Listen to me carefully, and don't interrupt me. Fritz and a couple of his asshole friends are here watching us. The minute you reach out and touch me, they're going to grab you and pants you."

At that point I went into emotional overload, and missed what he said next. Was he really telling me that this whole thing was a trap to humiliate me? I tried to snap out of shock, and hear what he was saying.

"So when I count three, I want you to run with me as fast as you fucking can. Run like your ass is on fire, do you hear me? Otherwise you're going to get the crap beat out of you."

It was like a nightmare but I couldn't wake up. What was I doing out here on the playground in the middle of the night? I didn't want to believe it, and Jimmy Kersher could see the denial in my eyes.

"Listen to me. Do you hear what I'm telling you? Don't screw up now. As fast as your fucking legs can move. Ready? One. Two..."

There was no time to wonder if I should believe him, or why Fritz would betray me. There was no time to explain to Jimmy that I didn't run, couldn't run, that I'd never run farther than the length of our driveway, that I didn't think I could run very far at all, much less run anywhere fast enough to get away from guys who wanted to hurt me, much less run as fast as he could run. I was not a runner. I didn't run. I couldn't run. Period.

"Three."

We both bolted.

I didn't hear the shouts of anger behind us until we were halfway down the block. I was running. I found myself gasping for breath, my arms pumping back and forth like pistons, my sneakers slapping down the sidewalk and across the street, charging up the hill, dodging between parked cars, lunging around the corner. Jimmy veered through a neighbor's yard and I was right behind him, zigzagging up a back alley, darting between houses and then suddenly jerking to a halt behind a garage.

There we doubled over, both of us gasping for breath, listening intently for any sounds of pursuit. The only light came from a streetlamp across the street. The only sound in the stillness was the wheezing of a bus a block away.

Not until that moment, gulping down the night air, trying to still my pounding heart, did I realize that I had, in fact, found some place inside me that was able to run. And not only had I run, but I had run hard enough and fast enough to keep up with Jimmy Kersher. I had run for my life. I had completely shattered my whole concept of myself. I was not too fat to run. I was not too out of shape to be good at physical activity.

"Come back here, you queers!"

We heard them following us for the first couple blocks, but they went right past us and we lost them. We stayed where we were, hardly daring to breathe, listening, but there was only the stillness of the night. The fun had gone out of the sport.

"Sounds like they're gone. I'm heading home."

He didn't say good-night, so I took a chance and just tagged along beside him. He didn't act glad, but he didn't tell me to scram. Together we walked the rest of the way to his house. He didn't talk, so I didn't, either. We just ended up walking together, not looking at each other, occasionally bumping shoulders, banging arms.

When we got there, he signaled me to be quiet, mimed someone sleeping, and pointed at a window on the side of the house. Then he guided me around behind the back porch, to a place where firewood was piled along with several cracked flower pots caked with earth. I thought he was leading me toward the sunken basement door. Instead he stopped and turned to face me, his eyes black and unreadable in the light from the porch. Then he put his back up against the wall and slowly lifted up his T-shirt, showing me his belly. I froze. The only sound was a moth banging itself to death against the porch light overhead. When I was too afraid to budge, he reached out and took hold of my hand and touched it to his bare skin.

He let me feel his belly muscles. He let me run my hand slowly down his front. Then he lowered his T-shirt and padded up the porch stairs without making a single board creak, keyed open the back door, and disappeared into the darkness inside.

I walked home in a daze.

PART FOUR

Chapter 24
Suddenly Last Summer

Horror stories and erotic games weren't the only torments to which I subjected my poor cousins. Frequently during those childhood years I put them through yet another ordeal when we were all stranded at Nana's house, waiting out the lengthy preparations for dinner. If you wanted to be included, then you had to be willing to perform in one of my dreadful little theatrical productions.

I was, of course, the writer and director who stayed safely off stage, gave the orders, and made all artistic decisions. They were my volunteer puppets, forced to wear silly costumes, memorize lines, sing, dance, and generally make fools of themselves. Sure-fire audience-pleasers were having kids portray their parents with gender-swapping, little boys portraying their mothers in lipstick and high heels, little girls portraying their fathers calling for a beer while watching football on television.

We would rehearse in the spare bedroom with the door firmly shut. We were very secretive. Adults were not allowed to interfere. Advice as to the time of dinner, or any scolding when we were being too loud, was transmitted through a closed door. The room would become stuffy and sweaty. We would incorporate any little songs or tricks my cousins happened to have learned.

Our performance for the adults took place after dinner. At Nana's house there was an archway that separated the dining room from the living room. This became our proscenium. The adults in the dining room stayed seated, those sitting in front turning around their chairs. The living room became our stage. The kids pushed back the floor lamps to make sure no one knocked them over, switched off the dining room lights on our audience, and switched on the overheads when the show began. Actors entered from the hall. Hamming and ad-libs were encouraged.

Adoring parents and relatives stuffed with food and wine were an easy audience, particularly when watching their own kids perform. Since, no matter how bad it was, our little comedy was invariably followed by my father getting out his accordion and jubilantly rocking the house with everyone's favorite songs, I remember nothing but theatrical successes.

Was that what led me to read my first play? Or was it perhaps seeing Mrs Yorozu in *Teahouse of the August Moon*? Suddenly I couldn't read enough drama. I loved dialogue. I loved how characters revealed themselves. And among the plays I read, by Ibsen and Shakespeare and Thornton Wilder, slurping up as much as an eleven-year-old mind could understand of *Ghosts* and *King Lear*, was a fascinating, disturbing play by Tennessee Williams that became my favorite play of all, *Suddenly Last Summer*.

I loved the play without ever really understanding it. I was fascinated by the sexy, mysterious brother, Sebastian, and couldn't figure out why all the horrible island boys did such a terrible thing to him.

I read the play three times in a row.

Maybe a week after my midnight meeting with Jimmy Kersher, I stumbled upon a news release announcing that *Suddenly Last Summer* was going to be made into a movie, that Gore Vidal had been hired to write the screenplay, and that it would star Elizabeth Taylor, Katherine Hepburn, and Montgomery Clift.

Why was I home alone that afternoon? I can't remember. My father was working, of course, but my mother and brother simply weren't there. I had come home from school restless, maybe a little lonely, and unable to find the right book had been wandering through the house looking for something to occupy my mind when I realized I was a few issues behind in my reading of my mother's subscription to *Modern Screen*.

I grabbed the most recent issues and made myself comfortable. Getting lost in celebrity lives would be a relief. School had become a nightmare.

Every time I looked at Fritz now, he gave me a knowing smirk. I was embarrassed to see that I had served my purpose. Sandra was no longer a possibility, so my friendship was no longer pursued. That I had escaped that night must have annoyed him. I lived in fear that he was still determined to degrade me. I didn't give him a chance to explain or apologize or come up with excuses. I didn't give him much of a chance to say anything. I dreaded even going near him, less afraid of physical violence than of being shamed, my secrets paraded ludicrously before the eyes of my classmates. As it was, every time I saw him laughing in a group of friends, I feared that he was talking about me.

As for Jimmy Kersher, things had gone from bad to worse. Any possibility of knowing him better had been destroyed. Whenever we happened to see each other from across the classroom, he quickly looked away and pretended not to notice me. Feeling his belly muscles would remain a permanent blockade against any hope of friendship.

Sandra was just as bad. When our paths happened to cross at recess, she looked in the opposite direction and hurried off to join other friends. My little social universe had collapsed overnight into a black hole. Encountering Fritz or

Sandra or Jimmy Kersher no longer brought me any kind of joy. They were now bleak reminders of happy days that had come to an end. I had lost not one friend, but three.

Miserable and alone now in an empty house, in an afternoon that seemed interminable, I had finished reading every halfway interesting article in every magazine in Mom's pile by her armchair, and felt utterly and completely isolated. Reading the *Suddenly Last Summer* article one last time before tossing the latest magazine back with the others, to occupy my time because I had too much of it on my hands, I decided to do the right thing and look up a word in the dictionary that I had stumbled over in the article, a technical term in the news release that I didn't understand.

The living room picture window looked out on the usual gray drizzle, so there wasn't much of a temptation to go outdoors, but there was more light over by the wall-size pane of glass so I was in one of the two pink armchairs on either side of the window, sitting in it sideways, my legs hanging over the arm, three copies of *Modern Screen* at my feet. Open on my lap was the family's huge *Unabridged Webster*, as heavy as a small baby, lugged down off the high closet shelf where it was kept.

Except for the drip-drip-drip of the rain outside, the house was silent, just me and the dictionary. That's how I know I was alone: the television was off. In the soothing, unnatural hush, I was flipping through heavy handfuls of pages until I reached the letter H, searching for the word "homosexual."

When I saw what it meant, I burst into tears. To my horror, there was a word for my secret. I wasn't a space alien. I was a homosexual.

How could I have been eleven and not understood that word? It was a different era. And the definition I found was not complimentary. I was a disturbed human being in a psychiatric state. I was a malfunction. I was defective. I was a deviant person.

That word meant me. That five-syllable technical term was a label for people like me. Those secret things that I pretended didn't happen had a name, they had been clinically diagnosed and labeled. Boys who had thoughts like that for other boys, there was a word for that.

From that day onward I began to see my fascination with Jimmy Kersher in a whole new light. What I had mistaken for natural admiration, verging on adoration, a heightened awareness of the beautiful symmetry of him, was perhaps something a little deeper and more complicated than art appreciation, my first intimations of something I wasn't sure I understood very well called lust.

I had succeeded in getting my wish. I had touched his spellbinding body. But it had magically transformed me into a homosexual, and brought me no closer to happiness.

Chapter 25
In the Confessional

No one else was in St. George's Church on that sunny, bright Saturday afternoon.

In Seattle beautiful weather is an immediate mandate for being somewhere outdoors, and it felt like everyone else was. As I walked the six blocks to the church, the world seemed motionless and lifeless, every house on the street as still as a postcard. I was the only thing moving.

As I stepped through the heavy, soundless slab of door, my footsteps interrupted the solemn hush. The big modern-style church felt more hollow and empty than usual, as though it had been completely forgotten by everyone. At least I was spared any quizzical looks or uncomfortable questions. I hesitated in the back, wondering what I was doing here, why I wasn't out in the sun with friends somewhere, being happy. Because I wasn't happy. And I didn't know where else to go. The one person I'd trusted with my secret was Fritz. I didn't dare tell anyone else.

Late sunlight streamed through the stained-glass windows, dyeing the dust motes red and blue. I had the whole church to myself.

I shuffled sideways into one of the pews over on the side, lowered the kneeler and hunched forward over my folded hands. I was miserable, and desperate, and scared. I struggled against a huge sadness inside for as long as I could, then shed some tears, trying to do it silently, wiping them quickly away on the back of my knuckles in case anyone surprised me. I was ashamed of myself, choked up with guilt for feelings I had never examined until now.

I tried to pray. I didn't know what to ask for. I felt like God had betrayed me for no fault of my own, unfairly made me a bad person without my consent or knowing why. Suddenly I wake up and discover I'm a sinner heading straight to hell, not because I wanted to be, not because I chose to be. I always thought I was one of the good guys. I didn't ask to be on the other team! I felt like I'd been hijacked by the devil, taken hostage by desires that were planted illegally in my suitcase by someone else.

I don't know how long I was there alone with my own misery. At some point I realized I was no longer the only person in the church. Though I kept my back turned toward the door, I could hear footfalls and rustlings and whispers. People were starting to come into the back. A kneeler dropped from an elderly hand and thudded to the tiled floor.

Then Father Cornelius entered the church up front all decked out in his robes, genuflected in front of the altar, walked to the confessional, and closed himself up inside the middle closet. People started lining up outside the adjoining cupboards on either side, waiting for their turns to step inside and confess their sins. Not until then did it dawn on me that it was the weekly time scheduled for Father Cornelius to be hearing confessions on Saturday afternoon.

Maybe it was a sign. Maybe that was what I needed to do. I thought about it, tortured myself with doubts.

The lines dwindled. A glance at my wristwatch showed that there was only a half hour left before Father Cornelius would be through for the day. It took me another ten minutes to force myself to rise from my knees, raise the kneeler back to its upright position, crabwalk my way out of the pew, cross the short, tiled stretch of floor and open the door of the confessional. It was like locking yourself in the closet.

The shutter slid open.

I could see him on the other side of the grill, mumbling his prayers in Latin and making the sign of the cross in the air in front of him. When he reached the Latin words that I knew were my cue, I began.

"Bless me, Father, for I have sinned. It has been two months since my last confession. My sins are…" and I faltered. "My sins are…" I didn't know what to say, or what words I should use to say it, or what formula to repeat that could possibly lead to my problem. "My sins are…" I hadn't really thought out how I was going to present this awkward situation. I broke into a sweat, and for one terrible moment I considered flinging open the door of the confessional and running out of the church.

Finally I just blurted out, "I think I'm a homosexual."

The words seemed to ring out much louder than I intended in the tight confines of my little closet of sin. I wondered if any people might have entered the church and be praying outside waiting their turn, only to overhear my grim, shouted announcement.

Father Cornelius didn't say anything at first. I could hear him breathing on the other side of the wooden latticework. When he continued to have no response, I began to suspect that he had fallen asleep. Then he said to me softly, so softly that at first I didn't believe he had really spoken, "Tell me, did you pray to God asking Him to turn you into a homosexual?"

I gasped at the strange question. "No, of course not."

His response to me was so unexpected that I remember it as vividly as though it happened yesterday. "Ah, well! You see, my son, one of the conditions of sin is that you must make a choice. So since you did not choose to be this way, how can it be a sin for you? Consider it a gift from our Lord."

I was too desperately sad to comprehend what he was trying to tell me. "Gift? How can a sin be a gift, Father?"

"How can it be a sin if God made the decision, not you? The good Lord doesn't sin. He always has His reasons."

"But how can there be any reason for making me like boys?" I wailed.

Father Cornelius moved closer to the grill separating us, and spoke in a gentle whisper. "That is for God to know. Being different will make you think about your soul. It will make you question yourself. It will make you grow up. It will make you learn what loving really means."

But those reasons hardly seemed compelling to me. I was uncomforted. "It's not fair. Why did God do this to me, Father? I don't want to be this way. I don't want to be different."

"Ah, well, I think you have to trust God in this," he whispered. "We're not allowed to know God's reasons. What matters is that you respect them. He made you, and He knows what He's doing. His law is simple. Love your neighbor as yourself. Compassion for everyone. That is one rule God commands you to live by, homosexual or not. Do you hear what I'm telling you? Compassion for everyone. Friends, enemies, everyone. Love everyone, and you don't have to worry. You learn how to love, and the rest will take care of itself. Now, say five Our Fathers and five Hail Marys for the poor souls in Purgatory, and make a good act of contrition…"

I walked out of the confessional and out of St. George's Church more confused than I had ever been in my eleven years of life.

Chapter 26
In the Principal's Office

Monday morning Mrs Yorozu's phone rang during our daily half hour of journal-writing. The phone's startling jangle interrupted the hush of two dozen pens all confessing their innermost thoughts at the same time. I was very guarded about what I wrote. I was still reeling from my discovery of the term for liking boys, and didn't know what other dreadful secrets might come bubbling up out of my depths.

Trying to think of the right things to include in my journal entry, trying to write about anything but the changes that were shaking me up inside, I happened to glance up to find Mrs Yorozu looking directly at me while she listened to the tiny voice at the other end. She agreed several times with whatever the caller was telling her, then hung up the phone and gestured me to come up to her desk.

"The telephone call was about you," she said quietly, and then paused, giving me time to reply.

"Was it bad?" I finally managed to ask.

"I'm not sure," she answered cautiously, as though she'd been giving the matter some thought. "I don't really know what happened." She hesitated, then asked, "Have you been playing an unusual game at recess?"

I tried to swallow, and failed.

"Well, regardless," she said, seeing that I was having difficulty answering her, and assuming correctly that the answer to her question was affirmative, "the principal would like to have a word with you." She quickly affixed her signature to a pink hall-pass. "Here," she said, handing it to me. "He'd like you to report to his office."

A thick hush coagulated in the portable. My stomach knotting in dread, aware that the pens had stopped writing, that the eyes of my classmates on both sides of the aisle were no longer on their journal entries but watching me, I crossed quickly in front of the classroom toward the door. I seemed to hear the boards creaking underfoot and every eye boring into me. Trying unsuccessfully to not let the portable door slam behind me, I crossed the deserted playground like a man sentenced to face a firing squad.

I had fallen from grace. I had gone too far. Why couldn't I keep my crazy games to myself? This would not go well. My parents would be mortified.

The secretary in the office had clearly been told I was coming. As soon as I approached the counter, she looked up from her typewriter, removed her carbon copies carefully and gestured toward the principal's door. "Mr McGrath would like you to go right in."

Mr McGrath had his back to me as I stepped through the door, his broad shoulders filling a handsome blue-gray suit. He appeared to be looking at something intently just outside the window. I tried to see what it was, but he was too big to see around. He seemed to know I was in the room, though I hadn't made a sound. Then I realized he could see my reflection in the window glass. What he was watching was me.

He turned around and towered over me.

"Do you want to close the door behind you?" he said ominously, making it sound like a courteous question but really making my blood grow cold with grim presentiments.

I did as I was told.

"Do you want to sit down?"

I sat down on the edge of the chair, not daring to settle back, anxiously waiting to hear my judgment.

"I think you know why you're here," he said, pulling out his chair and sitting at his desk. "Smart people usually know when they've done wrong."

I was smart enough to know that much. I tried to swallow, and failed.

Mr McGrath drummed his fingertips on his desk blotter. His office smelled of stale coffee. His necktie no longer had its morning stranglehold on his throat, but had been pulled loose in vexation.

"I have to tell you how much you've disappointed me. Maple Elementary is a good little school, and I try to keep it that way. You've created an upsetting situation here, and I don't appreciate it. How could you possibly think that was a good idea, making jump-rope into a kissing game?"

"I didn't think about it, Mr McGrath," I said lamely.

"That's obvious," he said curtly. "I've already received two letters of complaint from irritated parents wanting to know why there isn't better supervision on the playground. And that's not counting the phone calls."

This came as a blow. I knew I was in trouble, but now I knew I was in *big* trouble. Who could have complained? What student had become so unhappy playing the game that they had tattled on us?

"You know what I told the last mother who called? I told her I don't think children should be policed. And I don't. Do you? Is that what you think needs to be done? I think children should be free to be creative and learn how to interact. Do we have to have adults supervising you out there, to make you use a little common sense?"

He sighed, paced the length of his office and returned to his desk, his hands knotting together behind his back. "All right, no more kissing games. Use your head from now on. You're making my job very difficult, young man. I expected better from you."

By the time I walked out of his office, I was devastated. I didn't get far before I ran into Craig Barker and Bennie Grimes, setting up athletic trophies in the front hall display case.

"Not looking very cheerful there, are we?" observed Craig, always the shrewd observer. "Coming out of the principal's office, and look at that sad face on him. Somebody's been a bad boy."

"What that boy needs is a kiss," said Bennie, causing both him and Craig to turn back to the display case, snickering.

I walked quickly past them. Far too upset to go directly to class, especially into the cheerful, perceptive presence of Senor Nogales, I detoured abruptly into the boys' bathroom, locked myself into a stall, wrapped my arms around myself in a desperate hug of self-condolence and fought not to break down in tears.

Chapter 27
In the Boiler Room

That's where the custodian found me.

"How long were you planning on staying in there, mister?" called Leroy Woolery from the doorway of the boys' restroom.

I had become lost in the stillness, staring miserably down at the floor between my shoes, and when I got sick of that, staring at the back of the stall door, picking at the splintered wood and flaking paint. I had been hiding there ever since the end of second period. His loud words boomed into the hollow emptiness of the boys' room and startled me. I was too scared to think of an answer.

"And stop picking at the paint in there," he added, as though he could see right through the stall door. "It's bad enough without you picking at the paint."

"I'm not picking at it!" I denied.

"Oh, is that so? Well then, why are there all those little flakes of paint down around your shoes, will you please tell me that?"

I swallowed my guilt down in silence. The evidence gave me away.

"I noticed you going in and you never come back out. I can think of nicer places. Can't you?" He waited politely for me to reply, and when I didn't, said, "Not to mention maybe going back to the classroom, where you belong. Don't you think they're going to notice you never came back? You can't stay in the bathroom all day. You got a problem, maybe you should go to the nurse."

He knew I didn't have a problem. I opened the stall door. He was a big man in overalls with a barrel chest and mocha-colored skin. He could see the tear-tracks down my cheeks. I was beyond pretending. My little world was coming unglued.

When I failed to summon up any explanation of my behavior, he went on, "You look like you're having one very bad day, young man. Well, let me cheer you up by telling you that your luck has just changed. You are now talking with Leroy Woolery, master-class handyman, who can repair anything that's broke and solve any problem in this whole school, so you are talking to the man who can help you."

The custodian gave me a huge smile, as though he were trying to burn away my tears with the sheer heat of his good nature. I would have smiled back, but there were no smiles left in me. He waited. I tried to summon up some kind of reason to justify myself, but none came.

I had seen Mr Woolery periodically at school, but usually in the background, as a peripheral figure while I was looking at something else. I had never heard Mr Woolery say more than three words in a row before. The few times I had heard him talk, he had spoken very softly, and only a syllable or two got mumbled before he ran out of things to say. The only time you ever saw him, really, was if you were late leaving school in the afternoon, you might see him beginning to mop the back halls.

"I'm waiting to hear how I can help you, young man. Either you are talking mighty softly, or the acoustics is even worse in here than I thought, or else there's something wrong with my hearing."

Words wouldn't come out of my mouth. Suddenly I was overwhelmed with embarrassment. I was losing every battle. I couldn't hold the misery inside any longer. And to make matters worse, I couldn't resist the custodian's kindness. His unexpected warmth broke down the last of my defenses. I threw my arms around him, buried my face in his big shoulder, and cried until his shoulder was wet.

If I was a little more than he bargained for, Leroy Woolery never let me know. He allowed me to cling to him until I had myself under control. Then he loosened my arms and peeked out the door of the boys' restroom to see if the hall was clear. He grabbed my hand.

"Where are we going?" I asked feebly.

"Just you come along," said Leroy Woolery. "You don't need no hall pass where we're going. I know exactly what you need."

He led me through a door in the hall I'd never noticed before and down a flight of stairs into the boiler room.

One wooden armchair and a footstool were surrounded by boxes of varying heights on which were placed a coffee mug, an umbrella, a clipboard with dangling attached pen, a folded-up newspaper, and a battered black lunchbox. He insisted I sit in the one chair. Then he reached in the lunch box and took out a warm bottle of Coke, popped the cap off with a little device that appeared in his hand, and handed it to me.

I stared at the bottle. Coke! All I could think about was the tooth in Mary Steinberger's science experiment. Then I took the bottle out of his huge hand and drank.

After a couple gulps I managed to say, "Thank you."

"You are most welcome." He nodded in acknowledgement, then leaned up against a box and folded his arms across his overalls. "Now, you tell me – what's the problem?"

I wiped my soggy nose on the back of my hand. "I'm too ashamed to talk about it."

"You got no reason to be ashamed."

I blurted out, "I'm mentally sick."

His eyes opened big and white in amazement. "What? You don't seem mentally sick to me. Who told you that?"

"And I can't play baseball."

"Why, boy, that ain't no crime to not play baseball."

"And my friends don't like me anymore."

"Why, that's their loss."

"And I make up bad games."

"Well, I don't make up any games at all, so there."

"You don't understand. I'm a big disappointment."

For the first time I glimpsed anger flash in his eyes. "Why, that's bullshit. Who told you that?"

"I came out all wrong."

"Wrong? Wrong?" That pushed his patience over the edge. "There's nothing wrong about you. I don't want to hear one more word of this. Now you listen to me, because I know how things work around here. You can't go hiding in the little boys' room every day. There's no place to hide, son, believe me. You're gonna need a better solution than that. There's only one person you can be, and you gotta be him. I know, I know, you can spend your whole life trying *not* to be him, but then you gotta die knowing you was never you. That's one big mistake you don't want to make. You just gotta be who you are, because you can damn well do that better than anybody else. Just be the best you that you can be, and see if that don't bring you peace of mind."

I sniffed up my nose and managed a limp, half-hearted smile. Then I tipped back my head and drained the last of the Coke.

Chapter 28
Enemies

In spite of the encouraging words of Father Cornelius and the comforting thoughts of Leroy Woolery, I knew that my Maple School status had plunged irrevocably overnight. My spontaneous, oblivious personality now had a label that incurred social contempt, and strongly encouraged my becoming secretive and inhibited. I became ashamed of my natural longings and inclinations. I became furtive when looking at other boys. I was an official outsider. I had been divested of my privileged status as normal. There would be no more reaching out to feel anyone else's belly muscles. I could no longer trust myself to be myself. And along with it had come a fall from security.

I could no longer blithely ignore the fact that I had made some enemies. My weekly book reports, my constant high grades, my disastrous performance in any mandatory athletic event, and now this breach of appropriate masculine conduct were sufficient to rub some people the wrong way. There were jerks and bullies and students who simply didn't like me, who suspected my motives for reading so much, and now they all knew something about me that gave them the power to make fun of me.

I couldn't be sure who was laughing behind my back, or would make me feel threatened on the way home from school. The sight of two or three boys walking toward me on the sidewalk would cause me to nervously cross to the other side of the street. I was no longer the untouchable, irreproachable honors student with straight A's. I had an Achilles heel now, a big festering blemish, and would have to modify my conduct accordingly. I had a bull's-eye painted on my back, a walking invitation to anyone who needed target-practice.

I no longer looked forward to the recess bell. All too often I would see Fritz out on the playfield, talking with other boys. Whenever he saw me, he'd point with his thumb in my direction. The other guys would turn around to find out who he was pointing at, see it was me, and then laugh knowingly. Knowing what? I shuddered to think what they knew.

Because I never found out who accompanied Fritz that night, I never knew who else despised me enough to help Fritz pants me. Anyone who would do something like that must hate me a lot. Were they still waiting to accomplish their degrading prank? Was it those two guys with him right now?

Or was it the guys he was with yesterday?

Or the day before? Every laughing face held a potential attacker. Every smile concealed possible hatred. Every burst of laughter on the playground seemed aimed at me.

As for Jimmy Kersher, he avoided looking anywhere near my direction, as though I'd vanished. He gave no indication he even knew who I was, and stayed very busy playing with other boys.

He was still a thing of beauty when he ran, those bigger-than-life strides, those flapping hands. I always turned to watch him. If he noticed me watching, he never acknowledged that he had an audience. He acted like I had turned into a ghost, like he could see right through me.

I never saw him talking with Fritz again. In the classroom they behaved as though they didn't know each other. Whatever happened between them, I never found out.

Several days later, as I was starting up the outdoor stairs to the boys' playfield, Fritz and two other boys already on the playfield above me left the cyclone fence where they'd been standing and gathered at the staircase top. They stood shoulder to shoulder, three wide, blocking my way. To get to the boys' playfield, I would have to go past them.

I stopped halfway up the stairs.

Fritz grinned, and called down to me, "Come on up, I'll let you feel my belly muscles."

I turned around and went back down to the lower playfield.

There I played tetherball so poorly the girls made me quit the game and leave. For the rest of the recess I lurked in the shadows around the portables, stranded, frightened by the bullies who had blocked me on the stairs, horrified by my own bungling performance at tetherball, waiting impatiently for class to resume, for the day to be over.

This new fear of being exposed and embarrassed in public was crippling. My hard-won confidence in running now became a survival tool, since more than once I was forced to run home after school, a breathless two-block sprint to avoid clusters of unfriendly boys loitering on the corner. Or I would take long detours until my pursuers grew bored waiting for me. I began dreading going out onto the playground for fear that some bully might be waiting to play a trick on me, that I'd be pushed around or made the butt of someone's joke.

To keep away from Fritz and his malevolent cohorts, I began staying inside during recess time.

Chapter 29
The Secret Recess Project

When exactly did I begin writing it?

Writing has always come easily for me. Writing school essays was effortless. At the moment I felt utterly helpless, unable to strike back at the jokers who were laughing at me behind my back.

So I wrote. Maybe that's all it was, a child's revenge. Maybe I was just being a little mini-Dante, getting back at those vile Florentines who treated me so shabbily and drove me into exile. Maybe I was just trying to make art correct the injustices of life.

Finally, I think, out of fear and frustration, I began writing down what I wished would happen. That has to be it. I wanted justice. I believed in it, and I wanted it to happen. I wanted the whole unfair system shaken. And there was a precedent in my imagination for that kind of writing. I knew the genre, the subject, the style.

I needed monsters.

I needed invaders from another planet to blast apart the unfairness strangling my unhappy life. I needed ruthless alien beings to take matters in their own hands, to commit the mayhem I was too civilized to inflict.

That first day it was just an idle thought in the murky back of my mind. Gee, what if this happened? What if that happened? I'd had many such daydreams before, and this was nothing more than another. I only managed to get down four sentences, merely the sketch of an idea.

Invaders – sure, why not? Invaders, yes, unstoppable and inhuman invaders, a fireball out of the sky, a death-ray, who knows what else, blah, blah, blah. I didn't think much of the stuff at the time, just corny special effects. I was always jotting down ideas. Ideas were like dandelion seeds They were always blowing all over the place, lots and lots of them. Most of them died.

On the second day, with no real intentions, I expanded each of the four sentences into a paragraph. That's all. It could have ended there.

But by the third day I had written four more paragraphs, and that's when I realized something was happening. I was writing something. I didn't intend to, it just started happening. I was sitting in a school portable, writing about that very portable being attacked by invaders from another planet. I wasn't really taking it seriously. I was only doodling, but all the same...

A few more paragraphs the following day, and half a page the day after that. I only wrote during recess, when no other students were in the portable. I wrote furiously through to the end of the week.

Confronted with the weekend, I realized I couldn't stop, took the story home with me, and down in my basement sanctuary, at my grandfather's old roll-top desk, I added a new beginning and then slowly, patiently rewrote everything I'd written before in my neat, perfect penmanship.

That Monday I could hardly concentrate on what Mrs Yorozu was saying, I was so eager for recess to begin, so that I could move the story forward. I was still writing when the bell rang and recess was over. I was stealing blatantly from the greatest tale of alien invaders ever written, but that didn't even occur to me. The story seemed to write itself, as though it were being beamed to me from outer space.

I listened, and wrote.

The only one who noticed was Mrs Yorozu.

At first she didn't say anything. She watched me, and smiled, and let me continue to remain behind in the classroom at recess, staying in the portable alone with her while she graded papers and corrected tests.

She understood young people and must have intuited that something had occurred on the playground. I suppose it was pretty obvious that I was hiding from something. But rather than pester me with questions or intervene, she had chosen simply to watch, to be ready, to be compassionate, but to watch. She respected me as an individual, and allowed me to be different. She knew I liked to write. She wouldn't be surprised at my writing during recess.

She watched me inventing my own therapy. She must have noticed that what had looked casual, if not idle, at first had now become borderline frantic. She was now watching a little boy for the first time possessed by an idea, trying to figure out how to get it down on paper.

I'll never know for sure what she really observed and what she thought. I was oblivious to her presence, no longer sitting with her there inside the portable, with the screams and shouts of recess in my ears, but fighting for my life in an alternate Portable Five where I was locked in a life or death struggle with aliens, whose deadly tentacles reached toward me through shattered classroom windows.

Then one afternoon during recess, on a particularly beautiful spring day, bright and breezy and irresistible, when she and I were the only two people in the portable and everyone else was outside lapping up the glorious weather, as I got up to sharpen my pencil, she closed the book on her desk and said quietly into the peaceful hush of our shared solitude, "You're certainly working hard on something, aren't you?"

I was caught off guard. I had a sentence half-written hovering in my mind, waiting to be written down. I should have realized that I was being a bit obvious, forsaking my daily doses of physical release to remain at my desk intensely scribbling away, filling page after page of lined paper. All I could manage to say was, "I guess I am."

She smiled kindly. Mrs Yorozu had a smile that was like a blessing. "Good for you. Is it a story?"

I faltered. I was afraid to talk about it. I had never even dared to talk about it to myself. Was I really writing a story? I was certainly trying to get something down on paper. It had a beginning, and I was somewhere in the middle, and I was definitely shooting for an ending. Is that what the something was? Yes, I could see that it was a story, all right, a scary story just like I used to tell my cousins.

"Don't worry, I won't tell anyone." She assumed that I was hesitating to tell her the answer. I wasn't hesitating. I was discovering the answer.

"It's a story," I admitted. "Yes, I'm writing a story."

That was the first time I clarified even for myself what was taking hold of me. A look of complete delight flushed Mrs Yorozu's face. She leaned closer to me, so that our noses were only inches apart.

"What's it about?" she whispered conspiratorially, as though the subject matter might be an incendiary secret.

I couldn't resist telling her. "It's about Mars."

Chapter 30
Mrs Yorozu Breaks Her Word

Mrs Yorozu knew the art of asking questions and listening to answers. Smart people always do.

Before I realized how much I was trusting my teacher, her gentle probing and careful listening caused me to drop my guard. I spilled everything. It all came rushing out of me in splattering disorder, nudged and prompted by her, as honest as my eleven-year-old mind could make it, how I came to be there writing my story. I told her about *The War of the Worlds*, both the comic book and the novel, and about Little League, about Sandra and Fritz and Jimmy, and the bullies on the upper playfield.

All she had really asked me was what I was writing so obsessively during recess. I don't know why I told her the rest. Somehow it all seemed part of the same story. I didn't plan it. It wasn't a confession on purpose. I was just honestly trying to explain to her why I was writing a story during recess. Sometimes when you trust someone, when you realize someone is actually paying attention to you, the words won't stay inside. They come rushing out of your mouth, whether you want to say them or not.

It only happened once.

The next day we went back to our routine, sharing the stillness of the empty portable, for the most part without either of us uttering a word. Mrs Yorozu spent the time preparing her lessons and grading exams, working her way through a desk piled with papers from both grades in Portable Five, all of them needing her personal attention, while I was busy channeling this mysterious story that was squirting its way out of me onto the page as fast as I could scribble the words down on paper.

Neither of us tried to talk to each other again. Occasionally one of us would look up from our work and see the other one looking in our direction, and then we would exchange smiles. Just smiles. Her smile not only radiated genuine caring, it also reassured me that I could trust her, that she respected my privacy and would protect my secrets.

And she seemed to be doing so.

For the first few days after telling her, she betrayed no knowledge of my secrets or any further interest in my project. She appeared to have forgotten everything I said. Her behavior toward me seemed so completely oblivious to all the secrets I'd confided in her that I wondered if I could have dreamed the whole thing.

Then without warning she broke her word.

We were just finishing a special shared unit on local history with both grades participating. A gloomy drizzle had been rattling rain on the portable roof all morning, and the overcast world outside the windows, though no longer raining, was dirty gray and dripping wet.

"All right, that's enough for now," she began, standing up from her desk. "Let's put away all our books and papers."

Of course, we did so immediately, even though it was an unusual time to be ending a lesson.

"Class, I've been trying to keep a secret, but I just can't do it any longer," she admitted, immediately getting everyone's attention, particularly my own. "What many of you may not know is that while the rest of you have been running and shouting and playing at recess, one of you has been staying behind."

Suddenly I couldn't swallow. I couldn't breathe. I couldn't hear what she was saying because my heart was pounding too loudly.

"One of you has been remaining inside this portable every recess. Why would anyone give up their recess time, you may ask. Because he's been writing and writing and writing. What could anyone have to write about through every single recess, you may ask. All I know is that it's a story. So now I would like to ask the secret young writer in our group for a favor."

Mrs Yorozu looked directly at me. One by one, the kids in both grades turned to look where she was looking.

"The whole point of writing down a story is to share it with others. Would you be willing to come up to the front of the portable and share with us what you've been working on so hard every day?"

The class clapped enthusiastically, especially the sixth graders. Maybe they thought it would be a good laugh, a hearty dose of silly kid stuff. Craig and Bennie couldn't stop cackling with eagerness. It would be so entertaining to watch me make a fool of myself!

Mrs Yorozu looked straight into my eyes, as though honesty mattered, as though keeping your word to an eleven-year-old counted for something.

"I hope you're not angry with me," she said at her most charming and sincere. "I know I promised not to tell anyone. But I think it might be something very special that we all could benefit from and enjoy. If you don't mind too much? Would you come up here?"

I squeaked out a word of agreement, a word of forgiveness, maybe just, "Okay." Then I slowly slid out of my desk and rose to my feet. Clutching my little pile of lined paper in both hands, each page filled from top to bottom with my immaculate handwriting, I sucked in my stomach and walked down the narrow aisle between desks to the front of the class.

Standing beside Mrs Yorozu's desk, I turned around and looked out at a roomful of faces, sixth graders on one side, fifth on the other, Fritz with his cryptic, carnivorous grin, Mary Steinberger with her wholesome scientific interest, Craig Barker and Bennie Grimes with glee as fodder for their slashing ironic humor, Jimmy Kersher staring into space as though no one were in the front of the room at all.

Standing there was the last place I had expected to find myself. Last night I had taken my story home and re-written the last three pages, smoothing out the gaps and changes. I wasn't sure how it was going to work. It might sound dumb. I wasn't sure I'd said it right. I hadn't even had a chance to read the clean copy of my story through from beginning to end. There was so much more work to be done on it. There were clumsy transitions, and a couple missing sections that hadn't been written yet, and…

But this was not the time for excuses.

Instead I planted both feet squarely on the floor, took a deep breath, cleared my throat, and announced in a quavering voice, "The name of my story is *Mars versus Maple School.*"

Chapter 31
Mars versus Maple School

Who knows what alien beings may be watching us from outer space? Who knows how long we will be allowed to go about our simple lives before a smarter, stronger race of beings decide they've waited long enough to take our planet for themselves?

They landed during first period. All of us in Portable Five were concentrating so hard on our math problems that, for once, no one was looking out the windows. No one but me. Since I had given up on ever hoping to understand numbers, I was daydreaming, looking out at the clouds, when something made a smoky trail across the sky. I tried to figure out what it was. It seemed to slowly be growing larger. It seemed to be heading straight toward us. Then I heard a sound coming out of the sky, a whistling.

The crash shook the playfield and rattled the portable windows.

For one split second after its earthshaking landing, no one budged. Then everyone started to talk at once.

"Please, will you all remain seated," commanded Mrs Yorozu. "Stay where you are, and don't move until we know it's safe."

No one heard a word. At least a dozen students left their seats and crowded around the windows. Only two dared run to the doorway. The first one there was Bennie Grimes, flinging open the door and charging outside to see what had fallen from the sky.

"It's a meteorite," he cried.

"No, it's not," said Craig Barker, who was right behind him. It was the first time in their lives that they had ever disagreed. "It's artificial. It's smooth as glass."

The huge smoking cylinder had crashed in the lower playfield, destroying most of the tetherball court and leaving a gaping pit gored into the asphalt.

"Boys, come back here! Don't go out there until we know there's no radiation," cried Mrs Yorozu, but Craig and Bennie had already leaped down the portable stairs and were making wisecracks and laughing as they approached the gaping crater in the middle of the lower playfield. Everyone in the classroom rushed to the doorway, crushing against each other, trying to see.

"Looks like your Dad has been barbequing again," said Bennie, pointing down at the smoldering cylinder in the asphalt pit.

"Looks like your Mom has been repairing the oven again," said Craig, going right up to the edge of the pit. "Look, it's opening!"

The lid screwed off and fell open. Out came slithering half a dozen tentacles like huge pythons. Suddenly there was no more laughter. One tentacle wrapped around Bennie's leg and jerked him off his feet. One wrapped around Craig's head, so you couldn't understand what he was yelling. Then both of them were dragged kicking and screaming down into the cylinder. The lid slid shut behind them.

I was paralyzed, more scared than I've ever been in my life, unable to believe my eyes.

While I watched, a metal contraption folded out of the cylinder. It opened up, extended upward higher and higher like one of those three-part ladders that keep opening up longer and longer, or a three-necked telescope unfolding to full length, straight up until it became a huge tripod that was at least three-storeys tall, like three telephone poles tied together at the top. This colossal machine from Mars towered over Maple School on three hundred-feet-long metal legs.

A light snapped on at the top, like a single blazing eye. The Martian machine was so smart, it seemed to be alive.

It turned to look as, far below the tripod, out of the main building of Maple School came Mr McGrath, bravely waving over his head his white handkerchief tied to a yardstick as a sign of non-aggression.

"We are peaceful, civilized people here," he said into his megaphone. "Those boys must be released immediately." The principal of Maple Elementary brave approached the tripod. "You've caused a great deal of damage, and we're very disappointed in you," he spoke into his megaphone. "Now, return those boys at once."

In answer, out of the single eye in the tripod's head-like compartment blasted a blinding white ray.

ZAM!

Mr McGrath went up in flames.

"Close the door!" cried Mrs Yorozu. "Everyone, get under your desks. It's the only place you'll have any protection."

Some lucky ones obeyed her. Some, like me, couldn't turn away from watching the principal burn up – the sight was so horrible I've been trying to forget it ever since. Mrs Yorozu rushed up to the partially-open doorway and tried to pull me back into the portable, and so she was there beside me when a figure appeared at the far entrance to the playfield in the long gold-and-white robes of a priest.

"Mercy, space brothers!" cried Father Cornelius, his arms raised toward the invaders. "We wish you no harm. Come in peace. Compassion for everyone."

"Father, stay away!" cried Mrs Yorozu, waving her arms in warning, but it was too late.

ZAM!

Another white death-ray seered the entrance to the playfield, scorching the priest to ashes before he could say one more word, and melting the cyclone fence on either side of the stairs into metal puddles.

Screams and cries rang out from Maple School. The tripod took an enormous step, and one of its metal legs came down on Portable One, smashing through the roof and resulting in devastation and injury. Out of the tripod's eye came the white-hot death-ray, straight at Portable Two.

ZAM!

The south wall went up in flames. Screams came from inside, from students who were trapped.

Another blazing death-ray shot out of the tripod's head, and this one shot between Portable Three and Portable Four, striking one of the houses across the street.

ZAM!

I knew that house – it was where David Starr lived. I could see the bedroom window where I had read so many science fiction stories, a bedroom with shelves and shelves filled with paperbacks all going up in a blinding flash, his rows of science fiction magazines tumbling into a flaming inferno.

I was so scared my legs went limp. My feet wouldn't move. I tried to get back to my desk but I couldn't keep my balance. I staggered and fell over, hitting my head. There was a horrible cracking sound, like an egg being snapped in two, and the room spun around.

Someone started pounding on the door of Portable Five. Mrs Yorozu bravely opened it. In rushed Sandra Bergamini, her sleeves and best school dress torn and blackened from all the damage outside.

"You're not safe out here!" cried Sandra. "They've already smashed Portable One to pieces, and they've set fire to Portable Two." Then Sandra must have seen me lying there, because her screaming my name is the first thing I remember. Her next words were to everyone else. "Leave now. While you can. Before they cook you alive. You've got to get over to the main schoolhouse while you can still cross the lower playfield, before it's too late."

Unfortunately, it was already too late. The window behind the desk exploded inward. Sandra screamed again. A long tentacle swiftly slid through the opening, and across the floor. Sandra dragged me out of its way.

Mrs Yorozu was not as lucky. Before she could make a single cry, the tentacle wrapped itself around her waist and lifted her up...

Chapter 32
The Interrupting Bell

R-r-r-r-r-r-r-r-r-ring!

It broke my sentence right in half. The one thing I hadn't counted on was the time factor. I had no idea how long my story would take to read aloud, because I had never considered doing such a thing. I didn't have a clue how much time had passed. I'd been in a trance since I'd started reading it, and never stopped to consider whether I'd be able to finish reading it before the recess bell rang.

The spell was utterly broken.

The story was ruined.

Hardly able to conceal my enormous disappointment, I managed to take a single step back toward my desk, ready to put my story away forever. Outside the sun was breaking through the clouds. The day beckoned, bright and fresh and free. The door of the portable cried out to be flung open. Recess, glorious recess, was far more important than any ridiculous story…

Unexpectedly Bill and Benita both rose up out of their seats right in front of me, blocking my way, with Eugene and Robbie and Doug right behind them. I made the logical assumption, that what had caused everyone in class to rise to their feet at once was the recess bell, the sunshine, the freedom to escape from being forced to listen to my story.

I stepped aside to get out of their way.

And instead banged into Madeline and Bernadette behind me blocking my way, because instead of rushing for the door into the playground, they were converging around my desk. I was surrounded. No one was rushing out into the glorious new day. My classmates appeared to be intent on staying right where they were indoors, laughing and clapping and excited, poking me and pulling on my arms to get my attention.

"How did you come up with that?"

"How long did it take you?"

"Where did you get such crazy ideas?"

"Am I in it?"

"Am I in it?"

"Who else gets blown up by the death-ray?"

"Does Mrs Yorozu get eaten?"

"What happens next?"

Their responses were overwhelming, exhilarating, addicting. Half the class ended up staying inside, not leaving the portable to go out to recess. They laughed over their favorite scenes, and wanted to know the name of the book by H. G. Wells. Craig and Bennie were in their element. They were celebrities. Craig took me aside and offered me two dollars if he and Bennie could escape alive from the alien cylinder. On every side I was bombarded with questions.

Classmates who seldom spoke to me showered me with praise and talked to me like I had always been their friend.

What I had taken as a spell-breaking interruption turned out to be the best thing that could have happened. From that day onward I would yearn to have that feeling again, a writer who snags the reader's curiosity, who baits the reader with provocative teases, who grips the reader's interest and won't let go, a writer who sees his audience transported by the sensations generated by his story, an audience eager to know what happens next.

I would be trying to recapture that feeling for the rest of my life.

The bell rang. Recess was over.

Everyone rushed back to their seats. Amid the scrambling of feet, stranded again at the front of the room, I nervously looked down at the pages clutched in my hand, making sure they were all in the right order, hoping my revisions made sense, trying to find where I had stopped reading…

Chapter 33
*Mars versus Maple School (*continued)

...and lifted her up until she nearly banged into the portable's low ceiling. Mrs Yorozu's feet kicked in the air, no longer in contact with the floor. She tried to scream, but the tentacle was squeezing her so tightly that no sound came out of her mouth. She squirmed and tugged and struggled, unable to break free, while her class watched in helpless horror.

The door of Portable Five banged open.

Mr Trimm rushed into the portable, his jacket off, his necktie swinging loose, his collar unbuttoned, the sleeves of his white shirt rolled up, gripping the ax from the fire alarm box in the school lobby. He brought it down with all his strength on the tentacle gripping her.

Out spurted green blood.

With another chop, he was able to whack it in two, and pull Mrs Yorozu free.

"Stay away from the windows!" shouted Mr Trimm to the rest of us. "The schoolyard is crawling with them."

The row of fifth graders near the windows fled from their desks. And just in time, because another pane of glass shattered and a tentacle came bursting through, grabbing Jimmy Kersher by the arm and hauling him toward the broken glass of the window frame.

"Jimmy!" cried Mrs Yorozu.

There wasn't a single sharp object on her desk except a pencil, so she grabbed that and stabbed down with all her might into the tentacle wrapped around him. The wounded tentacle flinched, and jerked. For just one second, it loosened its hold. But that was all the time she needed. Mrs Yorozu yanked him out of the tentacle's grip, hauling him just out of its reach.

"Get away, quick!" cried Mrs Yorozu, and he scrambled across the floor. Then she saw me over by the door and called, "Do we have a chance of reaching the main building?"

I opened the portable door to see if we could escape across the playfield. A tripod loomed overhead. As I watched, it turned its weapon toward Maple School. A death-ray shot out in a blinding white beam. It blasted through the school windows. Flames shot out of the library. Mrs Hayes was inside, trying to put out the fire.

Mr Trimm cupped his hands around his mouth and shouted, "Mrs Hayes, get out of there immediately!"

"No, no, the books are burning!" cried the old librarian. She wouldn't leave her books. If they burned, she would burn with them.

Then David Starr lunged through the door into our classroom, gasping for air. "I've just come from Portable Three," he said. "I climbed out the window. It was terrible. They're from Mars. They're taking over the planet, starting here with Maple School." He tried to catch his breath. "The other students are trapped inside."

"We've got to help them," cried Sandra, and ran back out the door.

"Sandra, wait!" cried Fritz, and he dashed out of the portable after her. It was never clear whether Fritz was trying to go with her to help, or trying to stop her. Portable Three was blazing. She got there first. He could see her trying to pry open the door to help students who were trapped inside. "Sandra!" cried Fritz, but before he could reach her the tripod beamed down one of its death-rays.

ZAM!

Fritz was fried to ashes.

There were muffled screams from the students inside. From the window of Portable Five I could see Sandra helping some of the students trapped in Portable Three out the windows to the street. Beside me Mr Trimm was swinging his axe to chop off the tentacles that came through the windows, now on one side, now on the other.

"Only Mr Woolery can save us," said Mrs Yorozu. She had great faith in the custodian. "Is there any way we can reach him?"

"No one could find him this morning," said Mr Trimm. "Maybe the Martians already have him."

"The Martians will never be able to capture Leroy Woolery," said Mrs Yorozu with solemn confidence. "Never underestimate that man. He must be over there in the school somewhere."

"He might be down in the boiler room," I suggested.

"Yes, of course," agreed Mrs Yorozu, suddenly filled with excitement and hope. "That's exactly where you'll find him, taking his morning nap. He works very hard, and knows how important it is to rest."

"The phone isn't working," called Mary Steinburger. "They must have torn down the telephone lines."

"There's no way to reach him," said Mr Trimm. "It would be suicide for anyone to go out there."

"Not for me," said Jimmy Kersher. "I can run faster than those Martians any day. I'll run over to the main schoolhouse and get him."

"But, Jimmy," I tried to tell him. "Those Martian death-rays are faster than anyone can run."

"I'm faster," said Jimmy Kersher. "I'll get over to the school and tell Mr Woolery we desperately need him."

Jimmy bravely opened the door to Portable Five, waited until the gigantic tripod was looking in the other direction, and then took off racing across the playground. The tripod turned.

The death-ray shot at him.

Jimmy zigzagged.

ZAM!

The death-ray shot again.

Jimmy zigzagged.

ZAM!

Faster than the Martian's deadly weapon, he had almost reached the schoolhouse when the death-ray shot off the corner of Maple School's roof.

ZAM!

The bricks fell into a pile of rubble. Jimmy vanished in the cloud of dust. Only one bloody hand could still be seen sticking out from under the debris.

What a sad and horrible sight! When I saw that, I knew what I had to do. Jimmy had taught me how to run. It was the only thing in sports that I could do very well. I had to try to save him. I ran out the door. I heard Mrs Yorozu shouting behind me, telling me to stop, but I didn't listen. I ran toward the wreckage of the school.

Fortunately the tripod was on the upper playfield smashing down backstops and basketball hoops. I ran to the pile of rubble and blasted bricks and debris, and there under some burned planks I saw his hand. While the tripod was looking the other way, I threw off the planks and freed him from the other stuff that had fallen on him. Then I helped Jimmy Kersher to his feet. He was weak and a little dizzy, battered and bleeding, but still alive. I got him to his feet, hooked one of his arms around my shoulders, and we made a stumbling dash toward the school door. The tripod turned in our direction.

Out shot its death-ray.

ZAM!

It missed.

I managed to haul Jimmy into the main building, where the death-ray couldn't get us.

"You saved my life," he said.

"You taught me how to run," I said.

Then I helped him get up on his weak legs and the two of us hurried as fast as we could down the staircase to the boiler room to wake Mr Woolery from his morning nap.

"It's the Martians," Jimmy and I shouted together.

"Don't you worry," said Mr Woolery. "It's your lucky day. I can solve anything. Now, stand still, mister Kersher, while I clean those wounds of yours. You look like you've had a pile of bricks fall on you."

"You better hurry," said Jimmy Kersher, "before Maple School burns down."

Meanwhile Coach Gabby had arrived early for baseball practice. When he saw that a big gray Martian that looked like an octopus was crawling out of the smoking cylinder in the playground, he grabbed his favorite bat, ran down to the playfield, and with a single swing he bashed in its head, making a nasty mess of green Martian blood.

But another one crawled out of the cylinder and came toward him, and another. They surrounded him. More kept coming. He was outnumbered.

Senor Nogales ran out onto the playground from the main building, dragging with him the school hose and cursing the Martians in the most fierce and expressive Spanish while shooting a blast of water up at burning Maple School to put out the fire.

That's when Leroy Woolery showed his genius for solving problems. He ran out onto the playground with canisters filled with germs from Mary Steinberger's science project. Jimmy and I were right behind him, each of us carrying another canister. Using a giant strip of rubber that he had been saving down in the boiler room for an emergency just like this one, Mr Woolery hooked the rubber strip onto what was left of the tetherball poles.

"This ought to work just like a giant slingshot," he said, and fired a canister straight at the tripod, hitting it right in the control-room head.

The canister exploded in a shower of germs. Jimmy handed him another canister, and he scored another direct hit. Then I handed him my canister, and he fired that one at the tripod, too.

My canister missed.

It missed because the tripod was falling. Two canisters full of germs were enough. There are no germs on the red planet. The tripod fell down across the playfield. The Martians were coughing up green blood and fell dead out of the cylinder, and the tripod exploded.

Cautiously the doors of Maple School opened. Out came the school nurse and the ladies in the office with bandages.

"Come on, let's go help the other kids," said Mrs Yorozu, and the students of Portable Five crawled out from under their desks. Together we all walked out into the sunshine, glad to be alive, and stared at the giant tripod lying fallen across the space cylinder in the gaping hole in the middle of the lower playfield.

The invasion from Mars had failed. Maple School had bravely fought off the attack from outer space and saved our human way of life.

Chapter 34
Birth of a Writer

"The End," I said solemnly.

The burst of applause as I read aloud those two last words was so loud and so sudden that I accidentally dropped all the pages I'd been clutching in my sweaty hands. The sheets fluttered crazily to the floor. As I dropped to my knees to gather them up again, I could see feet sliding out from under desks. To my amazement, my classmates were all rising. It was a standing ovation. They were clapping and calling, "Author! Author!"

Both sides of the aisle.

They were calling for me.

I wiped my wet cheeks on my sleeve and stood up, shuffling the pages of my story in my hands. Jimmy Kersher was clapping. Fritz Wachter was clapping. Even Craig Barker and Bennie Grimm were clapping. They called out things to me that I couldn't hear or else I just don't remember, it was so long ago.

Mrs Yorozu was standing and clapping, too. Her smile was radiant. That's how I remember her, the teacher who changed my life, smiling her approval.

By the time I left Maple School that day, news of my story had already spread to the other portables. David Starr was standing at the foot of the portable stairs, waiting for me when the last bell rang.

"I just heard," he said, beaming. "You wrote a science fiction story. Will you let me read it? Can I borrow it?"

I didn't have to answer. I simply handed him the handful of pages. He snatched them with a cry of glee and broke into a run across the street toward his house, which had not been destroyed by a Martian death-ray.

When I got home that afternoon my mother was trying to iron shirts and talk on the phone at the same time without getting tangled in the phone cord. Bursting with happiness, longing to tell her what had happened, I had to be satisfied with giving her a quick kiss on the cheek as I dashed past her, bounding down the basement stairs.

I closed the door of my room and lay down on the bed, surrounded by walls of books, shelf after shelf of friends. So many people telling their stories!

Now I was one of them.